About the Author

Geoffrey Malone spent most of his childhood in Africa, where he managed to avoid any formal education until the age of eleven. After school in England, he spent sixteen years in the army, mis-reading maps in the Far East, Persian Gulf and Europe. He subsequently joined a Canadian public relations agency and worked and travelled extensively in North America. He became a regular broadcaster there and wrote his first book, *Brunner*, after discovering that a family of beavers were his nearest neighbours while living in a remote part of Ontario. He has two sons and now lives happily in London with his wife, a spaniel and a Norfolk terrier.

Also by Geoffrey Malone

Kimba
Brunner

Torn Ear

Geoffrey Malone

Hodder
Children's
Books

a division of Hodder Headline plc

To my Mother in loving memory.

First published in Great Britain in 1997
by Hodder Children's Books
a division of Hodder Headline plc
338 Euston Road
London NW1 3BH

10 9 8 7 6 5 4 3

A Catalogue record for this book is available from the British Library

ISBN 0 340 68295 7

Typeset by Avon Dataset Ltd, Bidford-on-Avon, Warks

Printed and bound in Great Britain by
Clays Ltd, St Ives plc

Torn Ear

One

Russet was hungry. More hungry than she could
ever remember. For the last three days and nights
she had stayed underground nursing four cubs, a
dog and three vixens, and waiting for Madoc to
bring food. Instinct told her to stay with them until
his return.

Earlier that evening, she had stood at the entrance
to the earth trying to find his scent on the freezing
night air. It was mid-March but there was no let up
in the killing frost that gripped the land. Behind her,
the cubs set up a wail of complaint which she did her
best to ignore.

She was a yearling and these were her first litter.
Their hunger seemed never-ending. They were
barely two weeks old but already the dog cub, Torn
Ear, had his eyes open. He had followed her up the

steep passage-way that led to the outside world and sneezed repeatedly as the cold air pinched his nostrils.

On a night like this, sounds carried for miles. Russet called again for her mate and listened intently. Earlier, a dog fox had barked a reply, but he was a stranger. There was no answering call from Madoc. She turned and picked up Torn Ear by the scruff of his neck and carried him back to the others. Then, with her own stomach churning with hunger, she lay on her side and let them feed.

Outside, the moon climbed higher and the frost deepened. It sparkled with cold fire and sent the pigeons, roosting in the great oak, huddling together for warmth. One of their number had already thumped to the ground, stiff with cold. The remainder puffed out their feathers and closed their eyelids tight to stop them freezing.

Russet stared into the darkness and let the cubs tug at her. They suckled in greedy delight. Afterwards, they lay with their paws around each other's necks and slept. And all the while she listened for Madoc's return.

He was strong and sharp-witted and walked with a limp, the result of an old shotgun wound. He was a survivor and had already lived for five years. He was wise and had taught her a great deal in the short time they had been together. But he was jealous of the dog cub and on his last visit had bitten him about the head. She had chased him out, then stopped the flow of blood from the cub's ripped ear with her tongue.

Since then, there had been no sign of him and she was close to starving. She was very thin and could feel the frost probing her fur. She shivered and pulled the cubs closer to her. She covered them with her brush and arched her body round them while they snuggled into her and fell asleep.

But Russet found sleep impossible. An hour before dawn, she could bear it no longer. She had to eat. Without food, she wouldn't be able to produce the milk the cubs demanded every two hours. She knew they were already beginning to weaken, as it was. She must get food and find it quickly. In weather like this, there would be a great many other animals desperate for food. There was no shortage of enemies both above and below ground who would make short work of a litter of unprotected fox cubs. A badger might, for one, and Russet knew there was a flourishing sett at the far end of the wood.

She got to her feet, shaking the cubs clear of her, and uttered a sharp, rasping bark to tell them to stay put. Then, ignoring their protests, she left them. She stood in the darkness at the entrance to the earth, waiting while her eyes adjusted to the glare outside. She listened for any sign of danger: and heard the soft rustle of a weasel running over ice-covered leaves.

Satisfied, she came out, marked the ground as a warning to other predators, then slipped into the night.

The ground was iron-hard and her tracks quickly lengthened behind her. In the moonlight, they were easy to see. She skirted a ploughed field and headed for the place in the hedge where she always squeezed through.

Another vixen had been here earlier. She recognised its scent at once. Russet hurried on. Beyond was a steep-sided valley covered in gorse bushes where there were several rabbit warrens.

The hunger inside her was now a constant pain gnawing at her stomach. She caught the sudden scent of lambs and stopped to throw her head back and pin-point the source. As she did so, she remembered hiding up in a thicket with Madoc the month before and looking down at the lambing shed in the field above Grice's Farm. They had waited in vain all night long for the men and the dogs to leave the place unguarded. The memory made her mouth fill with saliva and she ground her teeth together.

Abruptly she stopped, a front paw frozen in mid-stride. There was a sudden movement in the ditch in front of her. A rustling noise and a short terrified squeal.

A field vole shot across her path, its tiny ears flat against its skull. A weasel raced after it, chittering in triumph. A split-second later, the vole found Russet's scent and skidded to a halt. It began to shake.

The weasel seized it by the throat, cutting short its scream. But by then, Russet had tumbled the weasel over and held it pinned to the ground. The weasel twisted free and leapt at the vixen, slashing at her nose with tiny, razor-sharp teeth. Then it backed away, its eyes red with hate, and watched Russet eat the vole in one quick mouthful.

The delicious taste of warm blood only inflamed the fox's appetite. She licked at the frozen ground then searched the ditch, but found nothing more. She wasted valuable time nosing for earthworms and beetles, then remembered the unguarded cubs waiting for her and began to panic.

She came round the side of a clump of bushes and stopped. Below her she saw barns and the farmhouse built into the lee of the hill. Her nose wrinkled as she tested the air. Then her keen eyes caught a flicker of movement in the farmyard. Understanding came the very next instant, but by then she was already running hard towards the place.

The Grice children had been in too much of a hurry to get back to a warm kitchen when they had shut the ducks away the night before. The door to the run had not been properly closed. In the course of the night, one of the ducks had got out.

At first it had roosted happily on top of a bale of straw in one of the barns. Then it had grown hungry and flown to the ground. It was now standing on one leg preening itself.

Russet crept on her belly to within two metres of the bird. With infinite care, and never once taking her eyes off the duck, the vixen gathered herself to spring. Even as the powerful muscles in her hind legs bunched, lights came on in the farmhouse opposite.

Distracted, Russet seized the duck by a wing and

a frantic tug of war began. The wing bones splintered as the duck tried to escape, beating the ground with its good wing in a vain attempt to fly.

Russet went after it again. This time she grabbed it round the neck, cutting off its frenzied quacking. With the duck filling her jaws, she turned for home.

The kitchen door was flung open and two sheepdogs came tumbling out. A man's hoarse shouts followed them. Bright lights came on in the yard.

But by now, Russet was racing up the hill and careful to keep the cover of a hedgerow between herself and pursuit. The duck's body was warm and plump between her teeth and the taste made her senses reel. A fierce excitement gripped her, that gave her extra speed as she dashed for home and her cubs.

Not long after this, as it became fully light, a Land Rover drove up to the farm and a stocky red-faced man wearing leggings and a thick tweed jacket got out. It was Mills, the local gamekeeper, stopping by for his early morning cup of tea.

'That fox'll be back for the rest of 'em,' he told the

Grice family when he heard what had happened. 'You mark my words. Like me to have a look for it?'

Two

Russet raced through Potter's Wood. A song thrush heard her and complained noisily. Other birds, now alerted, joined the warning chorus that went in front of her. Russet ignored them. She squirmed her way through a tangle of brambles and dropped the duck at the entrance to the earth. She waited for a moment to see if she was being followed, then went inside.

Four hungry cubs greeted her. She licked them all in turn and stood there while they reached up to feed. But she quickly tired of this and, ignoring their protests, returned to the duck. She settled down to eat, holding it between her paws like a dog while she tore at the feathers.

The cubs followed her, protesting loudly. They stopped at the entrance, uncertain what to make of the outside world, and called to her. Russet could think of nothing but the need to eat. With eyes half-closed in pleasure, she crunched the bones to get at the marrow, then swallowed splinters and feathers alike in greedy mouthfuls.

Eventually, Torn Ear pushed past the others and tumbled down the steep slope to join her. Excited by the smell, he growled and worried at her jaws. When he tried to nuzzle her side, however, Russet cuffed him and spat out a piece of blood-covered meat. He smelt it all over then turned away and tried in vain to burrow underneath her.

When it was finally over and all that remained of the duck were its feet and its bill, she cleaned the cubs thoroughly, pushing them over on to their backs with her long pointed nose. She saw that their eyes were all open now. For the moment, they were all dark blue in colour. In a few more weeks, however, they would change to hazel.

When she had finished, she sat upright and groomed herself like a cat while the cubs played round her. They fought and tussled over one of the duck's quills, tugging and worrying at it. Proudly, Russet watched them and felt a glow of happiness spreading through her. She listened to the sounds of the new dawn but heard nothing to alarm her. She yawned and called them back inside. In less than half an hour, they were all sound asleep.

Mills the gamekeeper had the countryman's traditional hatred of foxes. Right now, he was worried. He had been so sure they'd cleared the place of foxes. He'd shot four himself before Christmas and after that put down plenty of poison bait in all the likely places. When the local hunt had last been here in January, it had found nothing.

Now it looked as if the foxes were back, and bold with it. Just the sort of vermin that would play havoc with the new batch of young pheasants he'd be putting down later in the spring for next season's shoot.

He had no trouble finding Russet's tracks in the frost. Casting round behind the barn a little while later, he saw the unmistakeable paw prints. They were the same size as a spaniel's but showed the two distinct pin-pricks of the front claws.

He followed them easily. As he trudged up the hill behind Grice's Farm, he remembered someone in the pub telling him he had seen a big dog fox lying beside the dual carriageway. But when Mills had

17

driven past the next day, he had found nothing.

He put a hand into a pocket of his coat and counted the cartridges lying there. He gave a little grunt and transferred the shotgun back to his right arm.

In the corner of a field, he stooped and examined a tuft of red hair caught on a strand of barbed wire. Mills squatted down and pulled it off. Looking out over the field, he judged the fox's progress. When he got to the far end, he found the place in the hedge where it had squeezed through. He also noticed spots of blood on a yellowed maple leaf.

As he came out of the wood, he saw that the sky was clouding over. There was a thaw coming and that meant rain. He quickened his pace. He had a lot to do that day and the thought of looking for a fox's earth in bad weather was not one he relished.

However, as soon as he saw the row of blackthorn trees on top of a steep-sided bank, he knew he had found the right place. His experienced eye noted the crushed grass and the narrow pathway through the undergrowth.

Mills gave a grunt of satisfaction, but went no closer. A breeze was starting up and he realised he was downwind of it. Instead, he struck out to one side and skirted round the edge of the thorn bushes and approached the earth from the rear, looking for an escape hole.

It didn't take long to find. He pulled a piece of thick netting from an inside pocket and squatted down. Carefully, he laid the net over the hole and pegged it down with small metal stakes. If the fox was at home when he put the dog down, he'd catch it here as it bolted.

Twenty minutes later, he made his way back to the farm and then drove off.

Russet lay in the entrance to the earth listening to the sounds all round her. Like all foxes, her hearing was very sharp. Somewhere inside the wood, she could hear a grey squirrel cracking acorns between its teeth. Nearer at hand, a blackbird was hunting for worms, rapping the ground with its beak. Rain was approaching fast and she knew that the worms would be tunnelling upwards towards the surface for the moisture.

The vixen yawned and shook her head to clear away any last traces of sleep. By now, it was early afternoon and hunger had again woken her. She preferred to do her hunting at night when the chances of meeting Man were remote.

But as the sounds of other animals all round her continued, she became restless. Her cubs were still fast asleep: she could hear their quiet breathing. Reassured, she decided to search the wood for dead birds and other victims of the recent frost.

She set off at a trot down the bank and through the brambles, following her usual path. Ten metres further on, something stopped her in her tracks. A sweet, cloying smell that clung to the grasses on either side. It was a scent no animal can ever forget. The fur along her spine lifted. It was the smell of death. A man had come this way.

The damp ground held the scent close to it and told her the man had been there some hours ago. A growl grew in her throat. She put her nose down even closer and, despite the feeling of utter revulsion, began to follow the scent. With increasing alarm, she realised it circled the area where she had her earth. Her unease changed to fear.

She stood there uncertain, full of conflicting emotions. Had she been on her own, she would have run off immediately and put as much distance as possible between them. Now though, she had cubs to protect. She went on following the man's scent. It brought her back towards the entrance to the earth.

As she approached, she saw Torn Ear standing in the path with his back to her. His good ear was pricked in curiosity. He must have followed her scent out of the earth and was now trying to find her.

She stopped and waited, watching him move forward again. Despite all the distractions surrounding him, she could sense his determination to find her. She followed, a couple of metres behind, proud of her cub until, unable to resist the tenderness she felt any longer, she called to him in a soft, throaty cry.

Torn Ear looked round. For a moment he stared at her blankly, not understanding how or where she had appeared from. Then he greeted her with a bark of pleasure and came running towards her. His excited yelps decided her.

The man would come back. She was sure of that. He would know where they were. Torn Ear and the other cubs were in danger now. She must hide them . . . and quickly! She picked him up by the scruff and, ignoring his protests, pushed her way back out through the brambles and away from the earth that was their home.

Three

They went at a steady trot through the wood and out past the badger sett at the far end. The badgers also had young. Russet saw the pile of freshly-soiled grass the sow badger must have dragged clear of the sett. Badgers were always changing their bedding, even when their cubs were house-trained. That was something she would never do. Foxes were not as clean as badgers, perhaps because they were more cautious by nature. No vixen would leave out evidence of her young for predators to find.

A magpie, turning over the heap searching for beetles, looked up as Russet went past and screeched in surprise. It took off in a whirl of black and white. The bird flew ahead and perched on an oak branch, calling to its mate to come and look. It was rare to see a fox in broad daylight at this time of

22

year. Soon, they were joined by another pair, equally curious.

Russet kept a wary eye on them. Had they been crows, she would have been even more cautious for Torn Ear's sake and taken to thicker undergrowth. Crows, with their brutal, stabbing beaks were not frightened by the size of any animal and preyed on the injured and the very young alike. Russet had found enough of both with their eyes pecked out to know what crows were capable of.

She took a firmer grip on the cub and lengthened her stride. She had made up her mind now. She would find the earth where she herself had been born and take her family there. If it was empty! It was a bleak place on the shoulder of a high hill surrounded by outcrops of rock and bracken. It was miserable in winter and food was often scarce. Rabbits preferred the lower ground where the grass was sweeter and the few hares that lived locally were more than a match for any fox.

But it was remote and far away from Man. The bracken would give perfect cover from watching human eyes until the cubs were old enough to fend for themselves. She paused to mark the ground again so Madoc could follow them if he wanted. She was too concerned about the safety of her cubs to worry much about him, just then.

She climbed steadily upwards for the next half hour. Bare rock began to show through the grass and the trees became smaller and twisted. Lichen grew along their branches. It began to rain.

She found the small stream she had been watching for. It tumbled down a steep valley in a series of waterfalls and flowed dark and strong through miniature gorges. Here and there, bones of long-dead sheep showed between the boulders.

It was a hard climb up to the overhanging rock where she had played as a cub, Below it, she was relieved to see the entrance to the earth was overgrown with nettles and bracken. The bracken smelt wet and musty. There was a small pile of broken snail shells on top of a nearby rock where a thrush had been feeding. But there were no other signs of life.

She put Torn Ear down and went to look inside. The earth was damp and the roof had collapsed in one corner, blocking an exit. But it was empty and that was all that mattered.

She called the cub to her and licked him and butted him affectionately with her head. She took his ear in her mouth and bit it gently in warning. 'Stay here until I return with the others!' was what she told him.

After she had gone, Torn Ear sat in the darkness just inside the entrance, peering out and occasionally whimpering to himself.

Forty-five minutes later, as she came back through Potter's Wood, something made Russet stop and listen carefully. The wood felt different. She tested the air, but the wind was coming from behind her and told her nothing she didn't already know. It took her a moment to realise what had changed. It was the silence. It was far too quiet.

That meant that every other bird and animal was listening too. But for what? Thoughts of the cubs waiting for her flashed through her mind. Russet went forward again more cautiously than ever. She moved soundlessly across the carpet of last year's leaves, her red fur blending perfectly into the background. The silent ghost of a dull March day.

She felt a sudden series of vibrations through her paws and heard the faint click of stone on stone, sounds that were inaudible to human ears. It was a pair of moles, hard at work digging new tunnels and getting ready for the birth of their young. Russet looked around to remember the place for the future.

A jay landed heavily in a bush beside her and mocked her with a loud screech. Russet looked up, sensing the spite in its cry. Other birds now appeared, mocking and jeering at her. Some even flew close to her head. Russet had never known birds behave like this before. They were no longer frightened of her. Confused, she ran on.

And then she heard dogs barking not far ahead and her tongue went suddenly dry. She crouched in a hollow under the roots of a tree, then squirmed forward on her belly. She peered out from under a bush. What she saw made her snarl!

A Land Rover was parked twenty metres away. Two small dogs, wild with excitement, were tied to the vehicle's bumper bar. They ran backwards and forwards in short dashes, straining to get free.

They were working dogs, bred through the centuries to hunt animals underground. Terriers, with scarred muzzles and strong jaws. Russet knew why they were here the moment she saw them. She howled a warning to her cubs to lie still, but it was lost in the noise the dogs were making.

There was a man standing on top of the bank and

another by the earth itself. The man by the entrance straightened up.

'Keep your eyes on the net!' he shouted. 'I'm putting Lady in first!' The other waved an arm in acknowledgement.

Mills walked over to the Land Rover and untied one of the dogs. At the entrance to the earth he knelt, holding it tightly in his arms while it struggled to get free. Then he half threw the dog inside.

The Jack Russell disappeared, barking furiously. Mills clambered up the bank to join a third man, who was lying full-length on the ground, a hand cupped to one ear.

Long before it was apparent to human ears, Russet heard the triumphant note in the dog's barking and the faint, terrified yelping of her cubs. She sprang to her feet and ran out into the open where the smell of men and dogs was overpowering.

It clogged her nostrils. Panic-stricken, she turned this way and that, her own fear too great to let her go any closer. The other dog saw her and rushed to the end of its chain, hysterical with rage. It stood on its hind legs, desperate to get at her.

Mills looked round, saw the vixen and swore in surprise. He scrambled to his feet, cursing himself

27

for leaving his gun in the vehicle. Russet watched him jumping down the bank towards her. She heard one of the cubs cry out in pain. Her nerve broke and she fled.

The keeper watched her go and gave a bad-tempered shrug. He went round to the rear of the Land Rover and pulled out a couple of spades. He flung them on to the short springy grass above the earth.

One of the men grinned. 'Lady's found 'em I reckon,' he told the keeper. 'Just listen to the racket she's making!' He scuffed the ground with his boot. 'Reckon they're just about under here. If they're little ones, she'll have had 'em all by now.'

'Start digging!' Mills told him impatiently. 'Let's just make sure.'

The moon was obscured by thick cloud and the wind had strengthened, carrying with it the scent of blood far into the night. In the bushes near the earth, the predators were gathering. But none of them, not even the stoat, dared go any closer while the vixen still pawed at the broken little bodies lying on the pile of earth.

Four

Spring was late that year. Rain dripped endlessly from a slate-coloured sky and the wind was bad-tempered and cold. April was almost over before the sun finally appeared.

Torn Ear sensed the change the moment he opened his eyes. He lay in the darkness wondering what was different. There was no sign of Russet, although her scent lay heavy on the ground beside him. He knew she must still be away hunting. He yawned.

Outside the earth, a bumble bee emerged from its hole in a grassy bank, buzzing with impatience. It climbed on top of a stone and dried its wings in the hot sunshine. Then it launched itself upwards, flew clumsily away.

Torn Ear sat up and listened. This was a sound he

had never heard before. He scrambled to his feet and ran lightly up the steep passage that led to the entrance. And here he stopped in wonder.

Outside, beyond the muddy patch where he usually played, was a world he had never seen before. He sat back on his haunches, blinking in amazement.

Every rain drop, every tiny spider's web flashed and sparkled in the sunshine. For the first time in his life, he felt the warmth of the sun on his body. He stared up at it in awe and yelped when it dazzled his eyes.

The air was warm and bursting with new scents. The sap was rising in the bracken, a strange yeasty smell that settled on the back of his tongue. White hawthorn blossom swelled inside a million buds, impatient to be free.

He closed his eyes and looked away . . .

. . . And looked back again. It was still there! A great rush of happiness seized him. He wanted to explore and play and live in this wonderful new place.

He ran into the open and scampered across the glistening turf. The sun winked at him from a large gorse bush. Torn Ear reached up and patted a spiky branch, then leapt back as the dew-drops fell in sparkles across his muzzle.

He did it again, growling in mock ferocity, and tried to catch the droplets between his teeth. A wren scolded him from deep inside the bush. She had a nest in there, with six tiny eggs ready to be hatched.

Torn Ear dropped to the ground like a dog and barked at her. The next moment he was off, chasing round the rocks in a mad circle. Round and round he went, trying to catch his small tail. Then he rolled over on his back and kicked his legs in the air. When he got bored doing this, he sat up and began to scratch.

High overhead and invisible to any human eye, a tiny black speck circled. From where it soared, the great bird could see over forty miles. It swung in a lazy circle, head cocked to one side, studying the ground for signs of movement.

It watched a red post office van drive into a farmyard and saw the dogs rushing to meet it. It studied the flock of sheep in the fields above, searching for sickly lambs. It dipped a wing and made a wider turn and saw Torn Ear. The bird's talons clenched and then opened more slowly.

Torn Ear had now found a piece of twig and was

31

playing with it. He held it between his front paws and started to tear the bark off in thin strips which he chewed. This reminded him that he was hungry. He began to complain, quietly at first, then in a series of sharp cries. Russet was not back, so he barked louder.

Russet heard her cub's cries and quickened her pace. It was almost five weeks now since that terrible day in March when the vixen had slunk back here, filled with a crushing sense of loss. But her joy on finding Torn Ear alive and well soon drove everything else from her mind.

In a frenzy of love she had licked him and washed him, tumbling him over and over again, ignoring his squeals of protest. By the time he had fed and fallen asleep snuggled tight into her warm body, most of the immediate pain had gone. Her own instinct for survival saw to that.

But if the intensity of the agony Russet had endured passed quickly, the memory of what had happened would never be forgotten. It was stored away in her experience of Man and his treacherous ally, the Dog. She would pass on that knowledge to Torn Ear, as he in his turn would to his own offspring.

Now, she was tired. It had been a long night. She had left the earth just after moonrise and almost at once found an injured bird huddled at the foot of a tree. It lay hidden in a drift of old brown leaves. It had tried to defend its eggs from a marauding magpie and now its wing was broken.

Each time the bird breathed, the wing moved a little. It was this faint sound that made Russet stop and listen and come stealing silently to investigate. She ate the bird in two gulps, leaving only the larger feathers behind.

She had then spent a frustrating hour listening to the mice scurrying deep in the bracken. The bracken was sodden and almost impenetrable by its roots. Russet could hear them squeaking to one another as they ran along their passageways. But by the time she managed to force her head between the tough stalks, the mice were long gone.

It wasn't until the sun was almost up and she was drinking at the stream to fill her stomach, that she saw the rabbit. From the corner of her eye she caught the flicker of movement. A young rabbit emerged from its burrow. It took a quick look round, then hopped across to a thick clump of grass on the bank above the stream and began to feed.

Russet froze, jaws half open. The rabbit was sitting up, using a paw to stuff grass further into its mouth. It was downwind of Russet and, besides, the noise of water swirling past must have drowned any other sound. It had no idea the fox was so close.

Cat-like, Russet began to stalk it. It was all too easy. The rabbit never saw her. And now she was bringing it back to the earth in triumph. Torn Ear's screams of hunger urged her up the narrow valley. She knew she had been away for much longer than usual and this made her hurry all the more.

She came out on to the bare hillside and stopped. The rabbit hung limply from her jaws, its eyes still bright with shock. She saw the rocky outcrop above their earth and started to trot towards it. A group of larks exploded, panic-stricken, out of the heather in front of her. They flew in rapid zigzags, calling a frantic warning.

Curious, Russet looked up and saw a huge bird of prey hovering high overhead. Her first thought was that it was hunting rabbits. Then, she had abandoned her own prey on the ground and was running, running for dear life.

There was a flash of red and Torn Ear appeared, running downhill to greet her. She could see the grin on his face. A shadow flicked over the ground between them. She shot a glance upwards. The bird was starting to circle. It was a tight, controlled movement as if it were marking its target.

Russet screamed a warning to her cub. From somewhere she found new strength and raced towards him. As if in slow motion, she saw the bird start to fold its wings tight against its sides. She screamed again.

For the first time, Torn Ear seemed to understand. He looked up and saw the danger hurtling down at him, claws outstretched. He yelped in fright, missed his footing and half-fell into a low gully washed out by the winter's rain.

There was an explosive bang beside him and the air was suddenly full of terror, flying stones and the smell of the hunter. The cub rolled over and over, desperate to avoid the huge beak stabbing after him.

Dimly, he was aware of Russet standing over him, snarling at the great bird. There were tail feathers in her mouth and a deep gash along her shoulder. The bird beat at her head with giant wings, then was gone.

Later, after Russet had comforted her cub, she went back to pick up the rabbit. But when she got

there she knew the great bird had taken it. A long
tail feather lay on the ground in its place.

Five

By the beginning of May, Torn Ear was the size of a small cat. He was weaned now and eating whatever Russet brought back. He was also learning to catch his own food. He had discovered that the black beetles that lived under the gorse bushes were very tasty.

Nine or ten of them at a time usually filled him up for an hour or so. When he had eaten enough he would play a game with them, flipping them over on to their backs and growling threats at their waving legs.

The game was to collect as many as possible in one place and then scratch earth over them. He would lie in wait for the first one to emerge and pounce on it. Russet was also teaching him how to catch earthworms, but so far he wasn't very good at it.

For the last three nights, he had followed her as she headed towards the clumps of long grass that grew at the foot of the boulders. Here she put her head close to the ground and listened hard. The milder the night, the earlier the worms surfaced. When they did, there was a dry slithery sort of sound followed by a faint pop as they emerged.

Russet tried to show him how to catch hold of the worm between his teeth without hurting it. The trick then was to be very gentle and pull it out of its burrow all in one piece. Russet tickled the sides of the worm with the hairs on her paws. After a minute or so of doing this, the worm would relax its grip on the sides of the burrow. She would then drag it out and eat it.

Russet took him with her now on most of her hunting trips and found he was a quick learner. Tonight they sat together watching an owl hunting over the hillside below them. The bird was beating backwards and forwards, head down, searching for food.

The owl was very old and its wing joints were stiff. That was why it was out so early. It needed time to make up for its painful slowness. It would be looking for easy prey such as a diseased rabbit or even carrion. Once on the ground, it would be vulnerable and no match for a sharp-witted fox.

Russet knew all this from watching the awkward way the great bird turned. Like all foxes, she could see as well in the dark as humans can in broad daylight. As it flew overhead she could also hear the brittle sound the wind made through its ragged feathers.

She looked across at Torn Ear to see if he understood the information she was silently imparting. In only a couple of months more, he would be leaving to seek a life of his own. The memory of what had happened to her other cubs made her even more determined that he should fend for himself.

Now, he sat beside her while she taught him how to watch and what to listen for and the meaning of the scents that lingered on the night air. Above all, she warned him of the dangers he would face in the nights and days ahead. Of baited traps and the cruel wire that lay hidden underneath. Of rooks and crows which would follow him across the open and betray his whereabouts to man.

Much later, she got to her feet, yawned and stretched. It was time to find food. Torn Ear followed her along a twisting rabbit path that wandered in and out of the bracken. The air was alive with the scurry of night animals busy with the humdrum of their lives.

There was turf underfoot, well-cropped by the sheep, and springy. Sharp-edged mountain grass grew in tussocks where the ground was boggy. Russet stopped and put her nose to the ground. Her eyes narrowed in concentration. She was listening for mice. Torn Ear copied her and almost at once heard the faint rustling sounds.

The end of Russet's tail began to twitch. Then she was springing high into the air and leaping all of four metres to land on top of the field mouse. There was a thump and a startled squeak.

Torn Ear ran to join her, whimpering for the food. To his surprise, Russet ignored him and quickly ate the mouse herself. Confused, he licked at the grass and the ground and caught a brief taste of blood. He snarled at her, demanding his share, but she turned away from him.

She caught another mouse a moment later and again ate it in front of him. When she finished, she licked her paws and yawned. When he reached up with his paw to get her attention she moved her head out of the way.

Puzzled and feeling very hungry, Torn Ear hesitated, unsure what was expected of him. The mice were silent now, listening intently. But slowly they forgot what had frightened them and began to run in and out of the roots again.

A metre away, he saw a grass stem shiver and heard the sound of squeaking. Torn Ear crept forward, his fur-cushioned paws giving no warning of his approach. With infinite care, he placed each hind foot exactly where a front paw had been. The sound came again and a surge of excitement carried him through the air after the scurrying mouse.

For a second, his tail beat from side to side, steadying him. Then he was on top of it, feeling it wriggling frantically between his paws. He bit down in savage triumph.

He caught four more before the ache in his stomach was satisfied. Then obediently, he followed Russet down to the stream, where they drank at the same pool. Later, he found some hatched bird's eggs lying under a straggly rowan tree. He sniffed them and licked the remnants of dried yolk.

Russet looked up, searching the tree. She sensed the presence of the mother bird and her young. She stood upright for a moment with her paws on the slender trunk and found the nest wedged in the crook of a branch a good three metres above her head. There was no way she could reach it. Had it been a bigger tree she would have tried to scramble up into its branches. Realising this, she began to shake the tree. Soon, it started to sway.

Torn Ear leapt up the steep bank to see if the added height there would help. Russet watched him with approval, even though her experienced eye knew it wouldn't make any difference. She had already checked.

Russet shook the tree again but the nest did not budge. The mother bird was joined by her mate and their frantic cries woke a neighbouring family of blackbirds. By this time, the valley was full of shrill alarm calls and every animal knew there were foxes about.

There was nothing to be gained by staying there any longer, so Russet called Torn Ear to follow her. A squirrel, out searching for a hoard of last year's nuts, heard the commotion and leapt back into the safety of a tree. He ran along a branch, furiously scolding the foxes as they ran underneath.

No one else saw them go. Slowly, the birds settled their feathers and one by one they went back to sleep. The moon began to rise and silence returned. By then, Torn Ear and Russet were miles away.

Russet led him down the stream and waited patiently while he clambered over the rocks. She saw how his paws were becoming harder. Soon, he would have no difficulty keeping up with her over the roughest country.

He had got his second wind by the time they came down off the hill. They ran through a copse of huge oak trees. Torn Ear had never see trees as big as this before. It was all so different from their own bleak territory.

A large moth came fluttering out of the darkness and flew into his face. Torn Ear snapped at it and missed it. He spun round and chased after it through the gnarled tree trunks. It flew upwards and he lost it against the grey bark.

He turned around, ran a few metres, stopped and realised he was on his own. There was no sign of Russet. He listened in growing wonderment. The sounds of a hundred strange animals filled his ears with a low murmuring.

The trees creaked and shifted their leaves as they settled for the night. A small animal was dragging itself across the ground and crying in pain. Torn Ear could hear the heavy tread of a badger moving towards it.

He shivered and fluffed up his fur, suddenly feeling nervous. The temptation to go and investigate was very strong. He was hungry again and the sobs of the wounded animal were making his mouth water.

But he remembered Russet's warning and stood motionless. He listened and watched and saw Russet waiting beside a tree, looking at him. With a yelp of relief he ran to her. She was not pleased with him for running away, and cuffed him. Chastened, he kept close to her as she led him out of the wood and into open fields.

They kept to the hedgerows where the wild pheasants nested, looking for eggs. Much later that night, as they made their way back, they heard the old owl hooting in triumph and followed the sound. They watched the owl land on a low stump and begin to eat a dead bird. When it had finished, it flew up into the branches of a hollow tree and began preening itself. Later, it went inside.

Russet waited for a while, watching the tree intently, but the owl did not reappear. Silently, the vixen went over to the stump and sniffed at the blood-stained feathers. There were small bones scattered in a circle and claw marks in the bark around the top of the stump.

She scratched at the ground and found a vole's skull in the leaf mould. She pulled it out with her teeth and showed it to Torn Ear. It was stained with age. There was an elderberry bush nearby with new growth sprouting upwards. She looked at Torn Ear and saw that he also understood.

Russet grinned and turned away. Dawn was coming. It was time to sleep. She called him and he followed her out of the wood.

Six

It was mid-summer. The spring had come and gone. Cuckoos had laid their eggs in unsuspecting nests and the hillsides were golden with gorse. The grass and nettles grew unchecked and gave good cover for a hungry fox.

Torn Ear was half-grown by now and his adult coat of red hair was rapidly thickening. His eyes were hazel-coloured and missed nothing.

He was becoming more independent and frequently slept out in the bracken during the day, some distance from the earth. He was expert now at catching mice and beetles but still depended on Russet to bring him more substantial food. When he had eaten, she would play with him, flicking her tail from side to side to provoke him.

Torn Ear would scream with excitement and stalk

the tail in a series of stiff-legged leaps until he was close enough to pounce. If he chewed too hard, Russet would scream at him or roll him over. Sometimes, she would let him win and lie on her back while he bit her throat. But he was getting too big for this and his teeth too sharp and needle-like for comfort.

The bond between them was a powerful one, but it was one that Torn Ear would break as soon as he was old enough to fend for himself.

He lay now with Russet under the spiky branches of a gorse bush watching rabbits pop up out of their burrows to feed. Some were only thirty metres away. Their white scuts bobbed behind them, inviting him to rush out after them. He had done that many times over the past couple of days and caught nothing.

He was secretly beginning to despair of ever catching one. Each time he failed, the worry grew in him. He knew that if he went on like this, he would be reduced to living off mice and earthworms. He would always be hungry.

Russet could sense the tension building inside her cub, but was not over-alarmed. She knew it was harder to run down a fully-grown rabbit than any other prey. He needed to be almost starving before he learnt how best to use his natural cunning. When that happened, she knew he would succeed.

The night before, she had returned home with a plump wood pigeon in her jaws. Torn Ear, who had only found a few beetles to eat all day, ran towards her, eager to share the meat.

She had snarled at him to keep away and when he had ignored her and tried to tear at the soft grey feathers, she had reared up on her hind legs. Then she dropped the bird in front of her and stood straddling it, warning him off with bared fangs. Bewildered, he pleaded with her, but she ignored him. Later, she had seen him trying to chew the bird's feet and knew he had eaten little since then.

Tonight he was starving and desperate to learn. A rabbit appeared right in front of them and calmly began to wash itself. It rubbed its paws energetically over the sides of its head and across its whiskers. Then it crouched down and started to feed.

Torn Ear gave a low moan and shifted position. The rabbit stopped to listen. Its ears flicked round a couple of times. It shivered and hopped away towards a patch of clover.

Russet took his ear in her mouth and calmed him.

She told him again that just bursting out on to an open hillside was pointless. There were always too many burrows that a rabbit could escape down where a fox couldn't follow.

No! The only way to catch one was to mark down an individual and then get within twenty body-lengths of it without being seen. That meant making the best use of cover and applying a great deal of cunning as well.

She wormed her way back out of the gorse and waited for him to join her. Then, quite casually, she went round the side of the bush and walked out into the open. Torn Ear followed in amazement. On all sides, rabbits sat up and stared at them.

At the top of the hill there was a line of trees. Without a backward glance, Russet set off uphill towards them. She walked slowly, letting her head droop. Torn Ear had never seen her do this before. He kept wanting to look over his shoulder and see what the rabbits were doing. Instead, he obeyed her silent command and kept right behind her.

The rabbits continued to sit motionless, eyes rolling in fright, watching them. When it became clear however that the foxes were not interested in them, they began to relax. Soon, a couple of the braver ones turned their backs on the foxes and started to browse again.

When Russet reached the tree, she trotted round behind it and immediately dropped to the ground. Torn Ear did the same. Russet nodded at him. Still lying flat, she peered round the trunk.

The rabbits had forgotten all about them by now and were busy eating again. For a while the foxes studied them, then Russet gave a grunt. Torn Ear followed her gaze. A young buck and two doe rabbits were leaving the main group, intent on feeding by themselves. They stopped near a tree about fifty metres away and a little below the foxes.

Russet noticed a fold in the ground leading towards it. Torn Ear saw it too. If they could only get into the depression they would be quite hidden. Torn Ear's eyes gleamed in sudden understanding.

Russet gave a low grunt and crept from behind cover towards it. Torn Ear followed, copying her movements exactly. Soon he was slithering on his belly across open ground towards the dip. By the time they reached the tree, his heart was pounding with excitement. The rabbits had not moved and were feeding with total unconcern. It was Torn Ear who noticed the nettles.

There were several small clumps of them strung out upwind of the rabbits. If the rabbits stayed where they were, it might just be possible to get in really close. He waited for Russet to make the move but she stayed where she was. She turned her head away and he knew then that it was going to be up to him.

He risked another glimpse at the rabbits and without further hesitation, crept past her. He reached the first clump and peered between the stalks.

While he waited, he noticed a hole in the ground in front of him and the steady stream of wasps flying in and out. It was a nest and he should have noticed it before. He had been stung by a wasp only the day before and the pain had been sudden and sharp. He had no intention of being stung again.

He crawled forward, the tip of his bushy tail flicking to and fro in excitement. As he peered out from the next clump, his heart lurched. One of the does was hopping straight towards him. Ten metres away, she stopped, uncertain. She sat up on her haunches, her nose twitching, scenting the air.

Torn Ear tensed. He hugged the ground while every muscle in his body bunched under him. He took a deep breath, and then like a spring snapping, he leapt out at her.

The rabbit screamed and jumped high into the air in terror. Torn Ear came leaping towards her. She turned to flee and as she did so one of her strong back legs lashed out and caught him a numbing blow on the nose.

Blinded by tears, he bit down a fraction of a second too late. He spat out the tuft of warm fur and in a skidding turn raced after the rabbit.

His claws ripped at the ground, his body pivoting to gain the extra speed he needed. He was oblivious of everything but the urge to catch the rabbit. Blood hammered in his head as he raced after the grey blur in front of him that jinked from side to side, desperately trying to throw him off-balance.

The rabbit had almost reached her burrow when Torn Ear exploded over her in a huge leap. The doe screamed again and skidded on her side through the dust and old droppings.

Torn Ear crashed down on top of her and seized her by the neck as she lay winded and helpless. She gave a great shudder and then lay still.

He carried the body back in triumph. It was a large rabbit and he had to drag it along between his front legs for most of the way back to the earth. He stretched out in front of the entrance and began to eat. He snarled at Russet whenever she came too close. He devoured everything except the leg bones.

Afterwards, he sauntered down to the stream and drank. He deliberately ignored Russet's call to join her and trotted off instead to his favourite place in the bracken. This was the happiest day of his life and he wanted to be on his own to savour it. After a while he fell asleep.

Seven

Torn Ear woke with the sun on his face. He lay perfectly still listening to the sounds of the morning. A family of moles was busy underground. He could hear them chewing through the bracken roots. Further away, he could hear the faint splash of the stream where it tumbled over the rocks.

He stretched, yawned and felt hungry. He did not want to go back to the earth and catch black beetles or wait until Russet took him hunting. He was bored with always doing that. Besides, he wanted to be on his own and hunt for himself. Now he could catch rabbits! There was nothing he couldn't do.

He pushed through the bracken and out on to the grass. He looked up and checked the sky. It was blue and cloudless. He began to trot, then broke into a brisk run. The turf was springy underfoot and the air smelt warm and inviting.

A blackbird saw him coming and shouted a warning. Torn Ear made a feint towards her, jumping up at the branch, jaws open wide. The bird screamed and flew off in panic. His heart leapt. A warm sense of well-being engulfed him. He was a fox. A young, healthy fox and it was time he explored the wider world.

He followed the stream down the hillside to the copse where Russet had taken him a month before. But when he got there, he chose a different path from the one they had previously taken. He ran hard and fast towards the fields and meadows waiting for him in the low country.

He leapt over a ditch and found himself in a field of cows. Curious, he sat down and stared at them. He was unsure about cows and didn't know quite what to make of them. The cows had seen him too and were already ambling towards him. They formed a circle around him and jostled each other to get a better view.

The boldest of them lowered their heads and came even closer. Their nostrils were wet and flaring and their breath rolled over him. Behind him, a cow snorted. Startled, Torn Ear sprang round and barked at it.

Some of the cows began to panic. Two of them took to their heels and the thudding of their hooves alarmed the fox all the more. He barked at them as loudly as he could and made a sudden rush at the rest of them. They shrank away and in a flash Torn Ear was through the gap they had left.

He came across more cows a short while later. This time, he stayed undercover and watched them. He decided they posed no threat to him. Their movements were slow and clumsy. They were of no interest to him.

He wrinkled his nose. Close to, the cow's scent was overpowering. It drowned everything else and clung to the ground like mist. He would remember that. It might just be important and he tucked the knowledge away for the future.

Not long afterwards, he saw two very different-looking animals. They were as high as a hedgerow and moved noisily. They stamped their feet down hard on the ground while they walked as if they hadn't got an enemy in the world. Man!

They were the first humans he had ever seen and he knew at once that they were dangerous.

He stared at them in fascination.

They were walking along a track in front of him, making no effort to conceal themselves. Torn Ear stood poised to run but there were no sudden shouts of discovery. He crouched under a thick clump of cow parsley and watched them approach. They came within twenty metres of him. Their voices sounded very loud. One of them dropped something on the ground as they went past.

When they had gone, Torn Ear emerged and very cautiously went to investigate. Head down, he followed their scent for some distance, memorising its oily sweetness. Then he went back to the cigarette packet. He studied it carefully but it seemed to have no life of its own. Daringly, he put out a paw and touched it and leapt to one side for safety.

He did this a number of times. Then, bored with its lack of response, he marked it in defiance and hurried away.

He soon found that there were fox scents everywhere and he spent a great deal of time examining them. Most of them were warnings to other foxes to keep away. Torn Ear knew this instinctively from their sour, unpleasant smell. They told him that the resident fox would fight any stranger, no matter what size, to defend his territory. The realisation made Torn Ear more cautious.

For the rest of the day, he lay up in a field of barley and caught the occasional field mouse who came too close. At dusk, he became more adventurous and ducked down into a dry ditch and ran along it. He took great care to listen and watch before moving into the open. Although he found several fresh markings on trees or gate posts, he never saw another fox.

On the second evening, he found a family of cubs. There were five of them and they were a couple of weeks younger than himself. They were playing round the roots of a large tree. He wanted to join in and called to them from across the field, but they were too busy to notice.

He ran towards them, barking happily. They saw him coming and huddled together, staring at him in silence. For a moment they all looked at each other. Torn Ear gave an encouraging little cry and dropped down in play in front of them.

One of the smaller cubs began to back away and half-fell into a ditch behind it. The dog cub suddenly spat at Torn Ear, who stood quite still, puzzled by their reaction. Becoming bolder, the cub made a stiff-legged rush at Torn Ear. As he did so, the others started screaming and hissing. Shocked by their hostility, Torn Ear was about to turn and leave when a tremendous blow knocked him over. The next moment he was fighting for his life. A snarling vixen almost had him by the throat. Her teeth raked along his jaw and bit deep into the fur at the side of his neck.

They rolled over, locked together in a struggling, spitting heap. Torn Ear lashed out with his back legs and caught the vixen in the pit of the stomach. She gasped, and for an instant let go of him. Torn Ear managed to throw her off to one side and heave himself clear. The next instant he was running desperately, too shocked even to yelp.

He found a thick bed of nettles and plunged into the middle of it. He lay there until sunset, shivering uncontrollably and fearful in case the vixen or her mate came after him.

Eight

He waited in the nettles until the bats were flitting through the trees before he came out. To the east, the evening stars were already bright and the air was warm and fragrant.

He caught a rabbit almost at once. It was a young one and had been browsing in a clump of tall grasses. The pollen must have tickled his nose. Torn Ear heard it sneeze and went to look. He ate it quickly, listening all the time for potential enemies. When he had finished, he smelt water in an old cattle trough and stood on his hind legs to drink.

Feeling cheered, he groomed himself. There was a tiny movement high in the branches of a tree. He stopped to watch as an owl floated silently down. There was a faint squeak and the owl flew back up to its hide with a mouse in its claws.

Later, when the summer moon made its dramatic appearance, he moved back into the shadows. He was so intent on keeping under cover that he didn't realise he was being followed. It was a shock when a large dog fox appeared as if from nowhere beside him.

Torn Ear froze. He had never met a mature male fox before. His instincts were to keep still and let the superior animal inspect him. The old male sniffed him carefully and stood for what seemed a very long time with his muzzle very close and above Torn Ear's nose. His breath filled Torn Ear's nostrils.

Torn Ear was only too glad to remain motionless. Evidently, this pleased the older fox. Quite suddenly he broke off, marked a branch lying on the ground beside them and trotted off without a backward glance.

If this had happened a few day ago, Torn Ear would have wanted to chase after him and be friendly. But that was when he was still a cub at heart. His fight with the vixen had changed all that. Now he knew differently. He was on his own.

The meeting with the big dog fox and his acceptance by such a powerful animal gave him a new confidence in himself. Torn Ear knew perfectly well that the stranger had not harmed him because he was not mature enough to fight him for his territory. Even so, he felt almost light-headed, as if he had come through a major test.

He began to explore, running silently through the woods, through fields of bristling crops, deeper into the unknown. Many hours later, he squeezed through a hedge and leapt lightly down a bank on to something that made him pull up short. Something he had never come across before.

It stretched away on either side of him as far as he could see. It smelt quite different from anything he had ever walked on before. Scents he didn't like. Smells that made the back of his throat feel itchy. He knew it belonged to Man.

It felt warm under his paws and in places was so soft his claws pierced it. He padded along, not knowing what to make of the sensation. The moon came out from behind a cloud and bathed everything in brilliance.

Ten metres ahead, the reflective paint on a road sign flared into sudden life. Startled, Torn Ear jumped backwards. To the fox it seemed as if an enormous eye was looking down at him. He turned and fled, stopping only when he could not see it any more. He was about to climb up the bank and leave, when he found a dead hedgehog.

He pawed at it, trying to turn it over and get at its soft underbelly. But he couldn't move it. Russet had taught him that the only way to make a live hedgehog unroll was to push it into a puddle of water. But where the puddles had been there was now only dust.

A little later, he discovered a packet of sandwiches lying on the grass verge. As he ate them, he heard a distant rumble, like the sound of a large bumble bee approaching. He ignored it and went on eating. He was beginning to feel weary.

He had not slept well since leaving the earth. He had at best been able only to doze, while keeping all his senses alert to any danger in this strange new world. Now, he had found the road and it was warm and strangely comforting to lie on.

A minute passed. He heard the noise again, louder this time and nearer, much nearer. He lifted his head and stared in the direction of the sound. The ground underneath him was beginning to tremble.

Puzzled, Torn Ear stood up. His ears were pricked forward, concentrating hard. He could feel vibrations through his paws. He thought he saw a sudden flash of light across the sky.

The noise was changing. It was getting very loud indeed. There was something else about it too. It was no longer a friendly buzzing sound. It had become an angry roar instead. Then he caught the smell.

It was a horrible smell. A burning, acrid, choking smell. Torn Ear growled at it, his hackles rising. And quite suddenly, something hideous with great glaring eyes came roaring out of the night straight at him.

He stood rooted to the spot as the Thing raced and bucked towards him. A storm of noise and wind and smoke blew him off his feet and sucked him underneath. He was on his back now, powerless to move. He lost consciousness.

It was dawn when he opened his eyes. It was drizzling and his coat was heavy and wet. He was cold and ached in every bone of his body. He didn't want to move. He just wanted to lie here and sleep and let Nature heal him.

The sound of an approaching car filtered his awareness. It was past him in a whine of tyres and spray before he could stagger to his feet. He saw the tail lights glare at him as he hobbled up the bank away from this terrible place.

He reached the safety of a field and leant against a barbed wire fence. The hills were black against the dawn sky. The shape of them was familiar. He suddenly thought of Russet and remembered her warmth. The earth would be dry and safe. He looked at the hills again to be sure they were the same ones and gave a whimper.

But when he at last reached the earth many hours later, there was no sign of Russet. Her scent was cold. She was gone. Torn Ear called for her continuously. His cries were caught by the rain and lost in all that greyness. He searched all the familiar places, but found no trace of her.

Finally, exhausted by everything that had happened, he went back inside and slept. When he awoke the next night, it was still raining. He went out into the darkness and sniffed the night. He remembered the big dog fox and growled. He knew now that he was entirely on his own.

Nine

Torn Ear lay hidden in long grass at the top of a bank. Below him, a farm track wandered between fields of barley and oats. The mud in the ruts had long since dried and the ground was cracked and dusty. A heat haze danced in front of him and he felt drowsy.

Later, when it became too hot, he would cross the track and make for the cool shadows of Potter's Wood. Or he might head for the river and lie up in the reeds. He liked the river. It was quiet and cool. There was also a pair of moorhens with an almost grown-up family living there. He had not yet caught one, though he had spent many hours watching. He was a good swimmer and content to wait until winter when the reeds would have died back.

It was over two months now since he had left

Russet, and he had wandered far afield. Some instinct, however, had brought him back to the area where he had been born. The original earth was now occupied by a family of weasels. He often passed it.

Life was much easier down here in the valley. Food was plentiful and the ground well-broken with copses and hedgerows which gave excellent cover. He had found a disused badger sett on the outskirts of a wood and slept there whenever it was wet or stormy. Otherwise, he was content to lie out above ground and sleep.

A loud buzzing noise close to his head made him open one eye. A bluebottle had blundered into a spider's web. He watched its struggles and heard its anger change to terror as the spider slid down towards it. The web shook for a while, then there was silence.

He stayed there for another hour. A farm cat sauntered by and bared her teeth when she caught his scent. She arched her back and searched for him with cold green eyes. Torn Ear stayed put until the cat's nerve broke and she turned and ran.

He watched her go. He had met her before and knew the length of her claws. He remembered too that she lived with humans and could not be trusted. It was time to leave.

He leapt lightly down the bank and headed for the stream. Although it was a good two miles away, he knew the ground intimately. He often covered twenty miles a night searching for food or exploring. There was not a ditch or field he didn't know in a five-mile radius of his own earth.

He knew the best places to cross a stream and where the undergrowth was thickest. He knew where he was by the shape of the trees and the way the land sloped. There was not a gate or wire fence he had not examined or a hedgerow he did not know a way through.

He only crossed roads when there was no alternative. The sudden rush and the smell of traffic terrified him. He had learnt to find long straight stretches of road where he could see and wait until it was clear. Above all, he remembered everything he saw and stored it away for future use.

A pair of crows followed him on lazy wings, hoping he would lead them to a kill. They lost him in the woods above Grice's Farm where he stopped and listened. This was where the gamekeeper kept his rearing pens. The wood was always full of the murmur of thousands of young pheasants. He could hear them scratching for food safe behind high fences.

There were strange scents in the air. New smells that brought the hair up along his back. He shivered. He could hear men's voices in the distance. Curious, he turned in their direction. A flicker of movement caught his eye. Two metres closer and he would have been on top of her.

A perfectly-camouflaged hen pheasant shot out in front of him and bolted through the trees. She had been lying in a drift of old leaves where even his sharp eyes had not seen her until her nerve gave way.

Torn Ear grinned but made no effort to chase her. For once he was not hungry and besides, he was keen to see what the men were doing. He skirted the keeper's hut. The man had come this way very recently and his dogs too. Torn Ear paused to identify them, then walked on. The men's voices grew more distinct. At the edge of the wood, he slipped under a holly bush and peered out. The men were only fifty metres away.

He recognised Mills at once, though the dogs were nowhere to be seen. But what held his attention was the other man, a man he had never seen before. A man on horseback with gleaming leather boots.

His nose wrinkled. There was something about the horse and rider that made him feel uneasy. Deep down inside him, the inherited wisdom of his species stirred. The horse must have caught his scent. It tossed its head and snorted and began to pull to one side.

The rider calmed him, patting his neck with a large hand. He looked around, gazing intently at the wood, then bent down towards the keeper.

'What's the betting then, Brian, you've got a whole family of foxes in that wood? Better let us go through it for you.'

'And have your hunt drive out all my young birds? Not on your life! My old gun's never missed a fox yet.'

'Makes up for everything else you miss, then,' the huntsman replied.

They both laughed. There was a sudden smell of danger in the air.

Torn Ear shivered and eased out of his hiding place. He ran back the way he had come. He went past the pens and the keeper's gallows, with its sad

70

collection of dead stoats and a freshly-killed magpie. The smell of its blood was strong and for some reason it unsettled him further.

There was something else worrying him. A nagging doubt that he was not alone. A feeling he was being watched. A sixth sense whose warning was growing stronger with each stride he took.

He looked back over his shoulder, scanning the trees. He thought he saw the lower branches of a bush move but couldn't be sure. He began to run hard. He dodged between the trees for a further hundred metres, then suddenly stopped. He caught a whisper of sound. A dry leaf rustling on a day when there was no wind. Now, he was certain.

He ran on and remembered a fallen tree he had seen earlier. Its massive roots would make an ideal hiding place. He was running as fast as he could and confident he was outpacing whatever was following. But he was curious to see what it could be.

He dodged round the tree and flung himself down. His heart was pounding while he waited, straining his ears to catch any sound. Not far away, a thrush suddenly shrilled a warning. Torn Ear tensed. There was a long silence. He began to wonder if he had been mistaken. Very carefully, he raised his

head. Looking back at him not thirty metres away was a young vixen.

Ten

Her name was Velvet and she was almost the same age as him. She was smaller and lighter with a rust-red coat and dainty black paws. As he approached, she crouched full length and raised her muzzle towards him.

Torn Ear hesitated. He could feel himself shaking with excitement, yet everything about his young life so far made him deeply suspicious. He was a loner. None of the foxes he had met since leaving Russet had been friendly. The vixens were not interested in him and, almost without exception, all the males were suspicious of a stranger and had warned him off their territory.

Velvet gave a whimper and arched her tail. He came closer and sniffed her face. She licked his nose. Torn Ear flopped down beside her, giddy with pleasure. He put his head on his paws and lay there staring at her.

She growled at him and flicked her tail. Daringly, he reached forward and prodded her with his paw.

She began to bark at him, sharp excited cries like a small dog, and half stood up. He darted at her, jaws wide in a huge grin. The next moment, she was leaping into the air over his head and racing off. He gave a yelp of excitement and chased after her.

Velvet broke cover and without a backward glance raced into the open. In front of them was a large field full of sheep. Velvet, with Torn Ear in hot pursuit, dodged and weaved between them, leaping into the air in sheer high spirits.

The sheep began to panic and run together in aimless groups. The man on horseback heard their bleating and spurred his horse to see what the commotion was about.

There was a wide ditch at the far end of the field which the foxes cleared in a graceful spring. Torn Ear, who knew the ground well, struck off to one side away from her. He ran well, his thick brush streaming out behind him. In front of him, the ground rose steeply.

When he reached the skyline he stopped to watch.

Sure enough, he saw her pace slowing and her head turning to look. A few metres further on, he knew there was a depression in the ground where she wouldn't see him until she was almost upon him. Satisfied she was following, he scampered on and flung himself down to hide.

As she came over the top, he leapt at her and the two of them tumbled over and over, screaming at each other and corkscrewing their bodies for advantage. Their fangs scraped together as they tussled and growled in mock ferocity.

Then, in a flash they stopped what they were doing and stood listening hard. They heard the thudding of hooves and the creak of a saddle. They looked at each other in surprise until the horse jumped into the field after them. They raced for cover as the solitary rider stood up in his stirrups and watched them go, his curiosity more than satisfied.

Velvet followed Torn Ear along the bottom of a deep ditch. He ran ahead. The ditch became very narrow and, in places, dense tangles of brambles grew over the top. It was green and gloomy down here with only the odd shaft of sunlight breaking through.

An inquisitive robin saw them enter the concrete drain that led under the road. They ran through a plantation of young firs, taking care to keep just inside the trees in case the man on the horse was still following them.

Torn Ear had never been chased by a horse before and was surprised how fast it could run. Until today, he had never met another animal that he couldn't outrun both for speed and stamina. He certainly had no fear of farm dogs.

He taunted them and played games with them, doubling back on his tracks and screaming after their retreating backs. The confused dogs would go round in circles, barking madly, and eventually giving up the chase. But a horse was a different matter.

When he was satisfied that they had given the man the slip, he took her down to the ruins of the old water mill, which was a favourite place of his. The millpond had long since become choked with rushes and water lilies. A tall canopy of nettles covered the ground and small bushes had taken root in the walls.

There was a brick wall he liked to stretch out on when it was sunny. It gave him a wide view of the approaches to the mill so that if Man did come, he had plenty of time to leave.

Torn Ear ignored the smell of moorhens which lay everywhere along the bank and picked his way through the rubble, carefully avoiding pieces of broken glass. He paused at the doorway and listened. The place was alive with sound. There were tiny squeakings and cries and the muffled scamperings of small feet.

Rats! Scores of rats with families of ten or a dozen to feed. Busy behind the brickwork and running under the floorboards.

Velvet pushed past him, her ears pricked. She snapped at a shadow that came out of a pile of rotting sacks in a corner. There was a loud squeal and the floor was suddenly full of rats dashing in all directions.

They killed a dozen each and then took the two biggest outside into the sunshine and ate them all the way down to their scaly tails. Torn Ear's muzzle was bleeding where a large female had put up a desperate fight.

He thought he had killed it earlier with a deep bite to its neck. It lay still and rigid where he had dropped it. But when he stooped over the rat, intending to take it outside to eat, it sprang for his muzzle and hung on by its teeth until Torn Ear managed to shake it off.

Satisfied, Torn Ear went back into the mill and selected the four plumpest carcasses he could find. He carried them outside, scraped a hole amongst the nettles and dropped them in. He kicked the soil back over them and thought it would make a splendid larder. He would return in a couple of weeks when the meat would be at its most delicious.

He wanted to show Velvet the earth he had made, but she yawned and refused to go there with him. Instead, they found a cool place at the foot of a tree and went to sleep.

When Torn Ear woke, the sun was setting and the first stars of the evening were already bright. He was aware that Velvet had left earlier. But her scent was still there, held by the warm ground to show she had been with him.

He followed her tracks and found the place where she was living. She had made a den under a bale of straw left from last year's harvest. Her scent was everywhere and he filled his nostrils with it.

Feeling happier than he could ever remember, he turned in the direction of his own earth and trotted off. He had met an animal he felt totally at ease with. Another fox who shared his own love of play and excitement. A vixen, about whom he already felt a little jealous.

Away to the west, the line of hills grew black against the sky.

Eleven

He did not see Velvet for two weeks after that, although he looked for her every night. He knew she still used the den under the straw bale. Sometimes he came across her scent while out hunting. Like him, she wandered far and wide.

Autumn had set in before he next met her. It was late in the afternoon, the sun a huge red ball in a misty sky, when she reappeared.

Torn Ear heard her calling and sprang to his feet. He went to the entrance of his earth and listened. He came out into the open and barked back. He saw two magpies and a crow circling above the ridge opposite. He guessed they were following a fox, hoping it would lead them to an old kill. He set off at a run towards them and very soon saw her.

He jumped high into the air with joy and ran

straight towards her, calling her name in short barks of excitement. She checked her stride, turned to look at him and came dancing towards him. Her eyes were bright with mischief as she leapt up to lick his face and tell him about the orchard she had found near the village where the men lived.

For the past five nights, she had been busy finding an earth. A special earth which would not just be for herself. Although she could not know it, Nature was starting to prepare for the birth of her first litter of cubs. She would be ready to mate in the first week of January. Before that happened, she needed to find a dry and safe place to live and then give birth.

Nothing now, though, could be further from her mind. She ran across the damp grass with Torn Ear at her side. They raced through the trees and only stopped when the men's houses came into view in the valley below.

Velvet made a wide sweep of the village, slipping past stone walls and the backs of cottage gardens until she came to a wooden farm gate. She turned and grinned at him and went through. The track beyond was thick with mud brought in by the farm tractors.

Torn Ear caught the oily smell of the machines

and hesitated. He had never deliberately been as close as this to Man before. To make it worse, there was still a little daylight left. Velvet, however, seemed unconcerned. He wondered how much she knew about Man, but he still followed when she looked back to see if he was coming.

She jumped up on top of a low wall and disappeared over the other side. The orchard was overgrown with enough cover to hide a hundred foxes. The grass had not been cut in years and the nettles were a metre high. Torn Ear began to feel better. He joined Velvet at the foot of a pear tree.

Windfalls and berries had been a staple part of Torn Ear's diet all through the summer. He had eaten crab apples many times and sampled gooseberries and wild strawberries. But he had never yet tasted anything like the pears, plums and apples that lay here in the grass, oozing with fermenting juices.

The last wasps of the year staggered drunkenly from fruit to fruit, sometimes falling over on to their backs, unable to take another step.

After a careful look around, the foxes began to eat. With eyes half-closed in pleasure, they moved from tree to tree sampling, comparing, devouring at a gulp the soft, squashy fruit. They ate like animals possessed.

And the longer they ate, the more they threw caution to the winds. They could hear dogs in the farmyard at the top of the lane, but thought nothing of it. Later, when the farmer drove in through the gate clashing the gears of his old tractor, they hardly bothered to lift their heads.

When at last they stopped, Torn Ear's muzzle was black with juice and his chest covered with fruit pulp. By then too, his head felt twice its normal size and his eyes were hot and hard to focus.

A moth fluttered past his nose. He knew it was a moth yet somehow it looked the size of a bat, which he knew couldn't be right.

He swatted it with a paw and to his surprise found himself lying with his face pressed to the ground. He wondered where Velvet was, but felt too tired to find out. He closed his eyes and groaned. His brain was reeling. Confused, he started to get up. He took a few steps, then slipped and fell again.

In the middle of the night, the rain woke him. Fierce, driving rain that lashed at his head. A cold wind blew it in slanting sheets across his body.

Feeling wretched, he sat up. His head ached and he desperately wanted water to drink.

He heard Velvet calling and saw her huddled up beside a wall. Together they made their unsteady way into the farmyard where the rain beat a tattoo on the corrugated iron roofs of the out-buildings. There was no sign of life anywhere.

They stopped to drink at a puddle, then splashed their way over to a hay barn. Inside, they shook themselves like dogs and groaned at the violent pain in their heads. The hay bales were stacked almost up to the roof. They smelt of wild flowers and sunshine.

With difficulty, Torn Ear clambered up the stack until he found a space where they could stretch out. Velvet followed him, and a couple of minutes later they were sound asleep.

There were dogs barking. Torn Ear whimpered in his sleep and his paws twitched. In his dream he was running in easy bounds, leaving them far behind.

The barking grew louder. He opened an eye and saw a terrier only a metre away. It was standing on top of a hay bale directly above the fox. Had it been a braver dog, it would have gone for Torn Ear's throat long before. Torn Ear sprang to his feet. A hay bale pressed against his back. There was no room for manoeuvre.

Another small dog appeared, barking furiously. Now, there were men's voices. The ugly sound of humans shouting to their dogs. There were deeper barks and a black labrador came bounding across the yard. It was broad daylight!

Torn Ear heard Velvet screaming at him to follow. He looked up and saw she was running over the bales towards the open side of the barn. He saw her jump down and disappear from sight. Torn Ear made a sudden rush at the terrier, then bolted after her. Behind him, the dogs were becoming hysterical.

The men had also seen Velvet. She was running daintily along the top of a high stone wall looking quite unconcerned by the noise. The farm track ran along the other side. The black labrador leapt up at her but fell back, a good metre short. It tried again and failed.

Torn Ear jumped down after her and followed. As he did so, a gun went off and the top of the wall in front of Velvet exploded into a shower of fragments.

A second shot crashed into the wall just below Torn Ear. He felt the stones shaking and almost fell off the wall in panic. He scrambled down the far side to safety and leapt the last metre. There was a plank of wood lying in the mud and he landed heavily on an upturned nail.

He gave a scream of agony as the nail pierced his foot, and he fell heavily on to his shoulder. The intensity of the pain was shocking. He rolled over on to his side, aware only of the nail driving up through his paw. Somehow he managed to free himself, using his back legs to kick the plank away. The nail came out at an angle and there was blood everywhere. Then he was limping down the track, unable to put the injured limb to the ground.

Through a mist of pain, he heard the men cursing on the other side of the wall and the sound of heavy boots running across the farmyard. He tried to run on three legs but knew it was hopeless. They would be after him in seconds. He must hide.

There was a dead tree further down the track. Its trunk and lower branches were curtained with ivy and old man's beard. If he could only reach it there might still be a chance. He licked his wounded paw to staunch the flow and lurched on. Anything to stop them finding him.

He pushed his head inside and used his shoulders to force a bigger way in. Each time he put any weight on his hurt paw, the whole leg buckled. Somehow he squeezed his entire body through and knew that in doing so, he had made himself a prisoner.

If they found him in there, there would be no way of escape. The ivy held him tight. He stood rigid with anticipation, waiting for the men and the dogs to come.

Twelve

The minutes crawled past. Nothing happened.
The terriers were still yapping, but now Torn Ear
could hear disappointment in their voices. They
were angry with the men for letting the foxes get
away. Eventually, the men shouted at them to be
silent.

A dog appeared at the end of the track. It was the
black labrador. Horror-stricken, Torn Ear watched it
through a small gap in the leaves. It stopped by the
gate that he and Velvet had ducked through last
night. The dog sniffed the gate and raised its leg.
Torn Ear heard the men calling and it trotted away
after them.

No one else came near. The men would not know,
of course, that Torn Ear was wounded. Besides,
being country people they would expect any fox to

be miles away by now. A door banged in the yard and silence fell.

Torn Ear waited until the throbbing in his foot became bearable and was just starting to back out of the ivy, when he heard a car start up. Moments later, it drove down the track towards him.

He remembered the way rabbits lay flat against the ground to hide, and shivered. He pressed up against the tree. The car came nearer. He could hear it getting louder by the second but he couldn't turn round to see what it was doing. If he moved, the ivy would shake and betray his hiding place.

The car drew level with the tree, went past and suddenly braked. A woman got out. Torn Ear watched in horror. The pain in his leg was forgotten in the face of this immediate threat. Somehow he had the sense to wait a second longer, and to his infinite relief, watched the woman walk towards the gate. She pushed it open and then drove through. The car disappeared in a cloud of choking smoke that hung in the damp morning air for a long time.

Half an hour later, Torn Ear came out of his hiding place. The sudden appearance of a fox set the birds off into a chorus of protest. He limped down the track as quickly as he could. His whole front leg seemed to be on fire. Pain came over him in waves every time he jarred his paw.

A blackbird fluttered ahead of him, betraying his slow progress with shrill cries. Grimly, Torn Ear followed.

His instincts told him not to go back the way he had come. Dogs would have found their old tracks by now and might be watching. He paused at the gate and looked all round him. Beyond the gate, ploughed fields stretched away as far as he could see. In the far distance, there was a spinney. He could see no cover of any sort.

His breath steamed slightly. It was getting colder. The wind was going round to the north. It was a long way back to his earth and the sooner he got there, the quicker he could nurse his wounded paw.

He set out into the open, his head turning from side to side, watching and listening for any sign of pursuit. He wondered where Velvet was. Perhaps she had also been injured and was lying wounded somewhere? The worry made him forget his own pain for a while. He trudged on.

He reached the spinney at last and with a feeling of huge relief stumbled into its protective undergrowth. His paw was swollen to twice its normal size.

His mouth seemed to be dry all the time now and he stopped frequently to drink.

Beyond the spinney, he was glad to see some fields heavy with kale. He made his slow way through the stalks, following the furrows. At times, his concentration slipped and he had to stop and remember the direction he should be taking.

He found a worm and ate it. That made him realise how hungry he was. His stomach began to complain. It came as a further shock to realise that until his paw healed, beetles and worms would probably be the only things he would be eating.

A heavy black wing brushed his back. He gave a bark of surprise and stumbled. A large crow landed three metres away. It folded its wings and looked at the fox from glittering eyes. Its mate, the female, thumped down beside it. Torn Ear snarled, showing all his teeth.

The crow bristled its feathers in a challenge and cawed loudly, mocking Torn Ear's helplessness. It stabbed the ground with its beak and caught an insect. It cawed again, took a couple of hopping steps to one side and launched itself into the air.

The female pulled her head back into her shoulders and made a short run at Torn Ear. He

91

stood his ground but could not stop himself yelping out loud. The female crow croaked in derision and ran at him again.

Distracted, Torn Ear only just ducked in time as the male bird came swooping down, aiming a blow to the back of his head. He snapped at the crow's legs, but it was out of reach. The female was back in the air and coming at him from the other side.

Torn Ear made a spring at her but slipped on the wet earth. A sharp blow hit him on the flank, then a vicious beak pecked at his head. The air was full of whirling black wings and hoarse screams. Another blow buffeted him and sent him staggering.

He was tiring rapidly and becoming confused. The crows knew that. They had been following him for some time, watching his limp get worse. They knew it would not be long before the fox made a mistake. When he did so, they would stab their beaks into his eye. That was a delicacy above all others.

Torn Ear began to panic. He put his head down and ran aimlessly through the shoulder-high kale. Every time he stumbled, the crows cawed in triumph. His ears were ringing with their cries when he slid head-first into a deep ditch that ran under a hedgerow. It was half-full of water and very cold. But it was safety.

The crows were furious. They beat at the branches above his head with powerful wings. Torn Ear sank down further and listened to their rage. There was nothing he could do to drive them away. He might have to wait here until nightfall. His eyes closed in weariness.

Thirteen

The crows lost interest after a while and flew off to their favourite tree. They sat in the branches bickering among themselves.

Slowly, stiffly, Torn Ear clambered out of the ditch. He was cold and bedraggled and his teeth chattered. He was still a long way from his earth. He found his bearings and hobbled on.

A mile further and the ground grew steeper. Head down, he plodded up the hill. There was a wood at the top. As he brushed past a low bush, a familiar scent stopped him in his tracks.

Clumsily, he hopped around to check. There was no mistake. He knew her scent too well. Velvet had stopped here earlier in the day. He was so pleased, he sat down and scratched himself.

There was a low bank ahead of him. It had once

been a wall but now moss covered the old stones. He saw an opening underneath a tree root and dragged himself towards it. A great weariness filled him. He began to shake from tiredness. The throbbing in his paw echoed his heart beat.

He went inside. Other foxes had been there before him but there was no further sign of Velvet. It was cramped but it was dry. He sank down and closed his eyes. He felt himself falling. It was a very long way down . . .

Torn Ear lay there in the darkness for two days and nights, while the fever took its course. He lay curled up in a ball like a cub, hardly moving. The gash in his paw became almost too hot to lick. He wanted water desperately, but was too weak to venture out and find it.

Eventually, when the wound had begun to heal, he dragged himself on his side to the entrance and licked at the moisture gathered along the tree root. Then he found a puddle. It tasted better than anything he could ever remember.

On the third night he woke, suddenly alert and knowing, even as his eyes opened, that he was better. He listened and sniffed at the air. There was another animal close by. He got to his feet. Gingerly, he put his injured foot to the ground and winced. But, it was nothing like as painful as it had been.

He walked to the entrance and found Velvet waiting outside. She licked his face and his ears. Little whimpers of concern bubbled in the back of her throat while he told her what had happened. She stooped to lick his paw but he warned her off with a low growl. She fussed over him for a while longer, then left.

She returned an hour later carrying a dead blackbird in her jaws. Torn Ear fell on it and devoured it with a cracking of bones. He was still hungry when he swallowed the last of it, but by then he could feel his strength returning.

Velvet returned the following night. Torn Ear was lying out in front of the earth enjoying the feel of a fine drizzle on his face. He watched her trotting through the trees towards him. Her head was held very high. She had an old buck rabbit by the scruff of its neck. Its back legs scuffed through the leaves.

She squatted down in front of him and expertly cut the rabbit in two with her sharp teeth. She gave Torn Ear half and ate with him. The taste of fresh blood brought strength flooding through his body. He devoured the rabbit in a couple of gulps and afterwards licked the ground, greedily.

Velvet stayed with him a while longer. Then, satisfied that he was almost recovered, she got up, licked his face and was gone. He called after her but she did not look back. Moments later, she was swallowed up by the night.

The next day, he put his full weight on the paw for the first time. All that day he walked up and down on it. As his confidence grew, he would break into short dashes through the trees. By nightfall, he knew he was fit again. His body felt stiff and cramped but it was nothing that a good run wouldn't soon shake out.

He decided to leave this place the next night and return to his own earth. He felt his old self again. He caught a grey squirrel and this pleased him. It had been too intent scraping a larder for some acorns at the foot of a tree to sense his presence. Now it had paid the price for carelessness.

He found Velvet's scent again and stooped to investigate. There was something else there. Something totally unexpected. But there was no mistaking its sour warning. It was the mark of another male fox, but a much older male than he was.

For the first time in his life, Torn Ear felt the rush of jealousy burn his face. At that moment, he became an adult. Although it was not the right time of the year for mating, he was already possessive. He snarled and heard the anger in his voice. He began to cast around, trying to find their trail. But it had long gone cold by then. He waited out under the stars for two more hours, listening hard. There was no trace of Velvet or the hated stranger.

He took his anger back with him to the burrow underneath the tree root and lay there with his nose between his paws. He did not like this strange, new feeling inside him which got worse every time he thought about Velvet. He thought about Russet too. He was missing them both far more than he ever had before. He felt miserable.

Towards dawn he fell asleep and dreamt that he was chasing a strange bird with a loud, echoing cry that he had never heard before. He woke, hungry as always but completely restored to health.

He licked his paw and found it hard and fully healed. He gave a growl of delight.

He went to the entrance where he stopped and

smelt the air outside. He knew at once that something was wrong.

Fourteen

It was a grey, misty morning with a raw edge to the wind that had the birds puffing out their feathers to keep warm. A heavy dew glistened on every blade of grass. Torn Ear saw a squirrel's tracks run in a black line across the front of the burrow towards an elm tree. He listened carefully and tested the air.

He could smell the gamey scent of pheasants on the wind. Closer, a mole was burrowing just below the surface. Torn Ear could hear it grunting with the effort. Moles were easy to catch, but not very tasty. There were the different scents of trees, but above everything else there was the unmistakeable smell of men and dogs. And something else. A smell that made his nose wrinkle while he tried to recall its meaning.

He heard a horse whinny in the distance and

stamp its feet as if impatient to be off. He remembered Velvet and the man on the horse. For some reason, the skin on his muzzle began to tingle. It was a feeling he had never had before. His ears flicked forwards in concentration. He realised there was not just one horse out there, but several. More were joining all the time, to judge by the sound of hooves.

He climbed up on top of the bank and looked around. He had explored enough of this wood yesterday to know the direction of his own earth. It was time to return there. He slipped into the morning and ran lightly between the trees. He heard a cock pheasant's distant call of alarm and stopped to listen.

Behind him, he could make out the faint sounds of horses on the move, the scrape of a steel-shod hoof on roadway and the creak of leather. He heard men's voices and a little later, something that made his blood run cold. It was the sound of hounds baying.

He stopped dead. It was a horrible sound that made him gasp out loud. The menace was unmistakeable. He gave a sharp yelp and took to his heels. Without pausing to look, he ran out into an open field.

A wild shout behind him made him spin round. He saw two men on horseback waiting by the side of the wood. Their pink coats were bright against the leafless trees. One of them stood up in his saddle, pointing at him, and shouted again. Answering shouts were already coming from further away.

Torn Ear took to his heels, furious with himself. Fool that he was not to have checked first! He raced away from them and a hundred metres further on jumped a shallow ditch into the copse beyond. He jumped up on top of a fallen tree and risked a look back. The men did not seem to be following. They had left the screen of trees and were out in the field, reigning back their horses and riding in tight circles.

Feeling very relieved, he ran on. He skirted a field. It had recently been ploughed and the earth lay in heavy, sharp-sided clods. He decided not to risk his paw trying to cross it.

At the top of a long rise he stopped, pleased with himself for giving the men the slip. It was a short-lived sensation. The mist was thinning out. Barely half a mile away, he saw the pack of black- and tan-coloured hounds. Behind them, a line of bobbing riders spread across the fields.

One of the hounds, sharper-eyed than the rest,

spotted him against the skyline. It threw back its head and gave tongue. Like a wave breaking, the rest of the pack took up the cry. He saw the hunt swinging round towards him.

Even then, Torn Ear did not fully understand the horror of what was happening. For a few precious seconds he stood watching them stream in his direction. Then it dawned on him. They were hunting him! As if he was a rabbit! He fled. For almost a mile he ran in a blind panic, not caring where he was going, knowing only that he must outrun them.

Only when he stopped to look back did he realise that it was his *scent* the dogs were following. He could run until his heart burst, but unless he threw them off his scent, he was done for. The ground was damp but the air above it would be getting warmer as the mist lifted. His scent would be growing stronger by the minute.

He fought to control his panic and scanned the ground ahead. He could make out the blurred shape of Potter's Wood. His eye tracked down its wooded sides searching for the old mill, but it was too misty to see that far. He did catch the dull gleam of water however, and recognised the river.

That helped to settle him. He was back in the

country he knew so well. Better than any man or dog. The urgent summons of the huntsman's horn broke in on his thoughts and he heard the cry of the hounds once again. That meant they were already over the crest, hot on his trail.

Torn Ear took up the challenge. He was a fox with the cunning of a thousand generations behind him. He knew he was running well, the soreness and aches already forgotten. All the time he ran, he judged where the hounds would be and watched out of the corner of his eye in case a rider came at him from the side.

Ahead of him there was a high wooden gate, with a gap to squeeze through beside it. Beyond was a ditch, where a small stream ran downhill towards the river. The water would help cover his scent. Torn Ear leapt down into it and splashed along. Behind him, the hunt followed on remorselessly.

He soon realised, however, that taking the ditch was a mistake. It was muddy and sucked at his heels as if trying to hold him back. It got deeper. In places it was choked with brushwood from recent hedging. He slipped jumping over a heap of branches and for a second lost his balance.

By the time he scrambled out, he knew the pack

was gaining. He pushed through a tangle of bramble bushes into a field. The shape of it was familiar and he knew it was the one where he and Velvet had played in the summer. The cows had been here recently and their scent lay across the ground in large oily patches.

The river was quite close now. He could also smell the mud and the moorhen's droppings. He ran for fifty metres towards the hedge on the far side of the field, then spun round and ran off in a totally different direction. He ran a further fifty metres at right angles before turning again. He did the same in another part of the field, hoping to confuse the hounds still more.

In the next field, he kept to the grass strip along the edge. A plastic shopping bag snagged in the lowest branch of a hawthorn tree marked the gap in the hedge. He slipped through and leapt out into the road. A man driving along saw him and braked hard. He banged a hand on the horn and stood gaping as the hunt poured round him a minute later in a cursing, baying flood.

Torn Ear reached the river, well pleased with his ploy. It should buy him the time he needed. He trotted along the bank staring hard at the water. As soon as the river bed became sandy, he splashed in. There would be no tell-tale muddy swirls left behind to show where he had gone.

Ahead of him, the trees surrounding the old mill loomed up. The mist was thicker here. He reached the reeds and pushed deep inside them. There was a sudden loud shriek and a frantic splashing.

A heron flapped away, beating at the air with outstretched wings, its long thin legs dragging behind. Horrified, he followed its flight. If the men spotted it, they would know what it meant. It reached tree-top height and was swallowed up in the mist. Torn Ear breathed again and sank down into the water to wait.

But not for long. Almost at once it seemed, the hunt closed in and the air was suddenly full of shouting voices, the jingle of harness and the smell of horse sweat. The hounds began casting round for his scent. He could hear them splashing and calling to one another as they searched.

A pair ran past him over on the far bank. He could hear the rasp of their breath. He sank lower, until the water came up to his jaw.

They spent thirty minutes looking for him while horses churned up the water so that it slapped against the bank. Through it all, Torn Ear remained motionless in the reeds, even when a wave splashed up into his eyes. Finally, the huntsman blew a single, long note and with much grumbling, the hunt began to move off.

Just then, there was a loud splashing and a man's angry shouts from very close at hand. An excited horse had stumbled and slipped down the bank into the reeds. Its rider was sawing at the reins, struggling to keep his balance. He pulled the horse's head round, clapped his spurs into the animal's side and urged it on towards Torn Ear's hiding place.

As the rider fought to control it, the horse reared up. Torn Ear saw the animal's front legs striking down towards him a metre above his head. Above them, he caught a brief glimpse of a man's angry red face.

He tried to get away but the water, for so long his friend, now held him back. There was a shout from the rider and the loud smack of the crop. But by now, the horse had seen Torn Ear and its plunging hooves missed him by a fraction. It reared up again and lunged twice, almost falling on top of the fox before it regained the bank.

Shaking with fright, Torn Ear listened to the

sound of its hooves fade and then waited for a further twenty minutes before he ventured out. The air and the ground reeked with the smell of the hunt. But they had gone! He had outwitted them! A glow of pride began to spread through him. He sat down and scratched himself.

Afterwards, he broke into a slow lope and headed towards his earth. He saw an old stone wall and jumped up and ran along the top of it in sheer bravado. He ran for a further two miles until he reached his earth. He gave a grin of pleasure and went inside. He fell asleep almost at once.

Some hours later, he woke with all his senses tingling. He lay on his side, listening. Then he was instantly wide awake. He could hear the huntsman's horn again.

He listened in disbelief, but there was no mistake. The hounds were in full cry and coming closer all the time. The horn blew an urgent series of notes. He was on his feet in a flash, peering out into the afternoon. His back legs began to shake and he knew he could not run all that way again.

He saw another fox not five hundred metres away. It was coming down the hillside in front of him. Even at that distance, he could see it was beaten. A fox with its tail well down. A fox caked with mud. A fox at the end of its tether. A fox he knew well. It was Velvet!

Fifteen

He watched in disbelief as she came down the slope. Her head was hanging and she was starting to roll with exhaustion. Even as he watched, he saw her lurch to one side, then recover. He knew then that she couldn't last for much longer. The ground in the narrow valley in front of her was marshy. It would be even heavier going now, after recent rain. That would slow her down still more. Once she had got across that, there was the steep climb towards the wood where Torn Ear was watching.

The leading pair of hounds was now on top of the hill. Behind them came a baying chorus. A couple of moments later, the rest of the pack and some riders on lathered horses started to appear. They saw Velvet and began to shout. Torn Ear could hear the thudding of hooves and the sharp crack of whips as the hunt piled down the hill after her.

In mounting horror, he measured the steadily-closing gap and knew the hounds would be up with her in only a few more minutes. But what could he do? He barked at them all in rage and dashed to and fro in front of the earth.

Velvet was two hundred metres away. She snatched a quick look over her shoulder and ran on. Below her, the horses were ploughing through the marshy ground, kicking up great divots of mud. The hounds were baying in triumph.

She was a hundred and fifty metres below him when Torn Ear could bear it no longer. A terrible anger drove him out towards her, screaming for her to follow him, trying to make himself heard above the clamour.

Did she hear him, or was it the sudden movement that caught her eye? Slowly, her head turned towards him. There was white froth along her jaws and her tongue hung slackly.

Three hounds were racing ahead of the others, hunting dogs in their prime with deep chests and massive reserves of stamina. They too saw Torn Ear and lengthened their stride. The huntsman's horn blew a frantic succession of notes. The horses stretched their necks out as their riders urged them on.

He reached her and ran beside her, urging her, encouraging her, cajoling her onwards. Fifty metres to the safety of the earth, but Velvet was slowing. Her eyes were almost closed, He knew that the slightest stumble would finish her.

In desperation Torn Ear left her and ran off to one side to distract the hounds. They turned their heads, howling at him and grinding their teeth. They were going to have both foxes, their voices told him. And very soon too. He could see the blood-lust in their eyes. He raced back alongside Velvet.

The earth was only twenty metres away. The entrance plainly visible ... Fifteen ... twelve ... ten ... and the nearest hound only four metres behind and gaining with every bound. He screamed at her for one last effort. If she failed, they were both lost.

Velvet fell at the entrance, the pain in her chest too much to bear any more. But the momentum was enough – just enough – to send her collapsing inside, leaving barely enough room for him to scramble in after her.

The jaws of the nearest hound snapped shut a

centimetre short of Torn Ear's tail. A terrible head thrust in after them. Fangs gleamed white in the darkness and the air was full of snarling and the hot stink of the dog's breath.

Loose earth began to sift down on top of the foxes as the dog fought to get its shoulders through the entrance. But the tunnel was too narrow. Baffled, the dog withdrew and howled its anger.

The foxes lay on the ground inside fighting for breath. Above them, the hunt was arriving. Torn Ear looked up at the sound of horses wheeling back and forth.

Slowly, he got his breath back. He leant against the wall of the small chamber and watched Velvet lying motionless. He leant over and licked away the mess from her mouth. Then he lay down in front of her.

Overhead the hounds surged and barked and tore at the ground.

Some time later, a Land Rover appeared and jolted over the grass towards the riders. It came to a stop and Mills, the keeper, got out. While he examined the earth, the hounds were whipped in. Torn Ear heard the huntsmen shouting and the sound of hooves overhead. The hounds protested at first, yelping in frustration as they were bunched together away from the earth. Soon, though, their mood changed and Torn Ear heard them barking excitedly.

Mills and his helper opened the tailgate of the vehicle and an excited buzz of chatter broke out at the sight of the two terriers. Hunt followers were also appearing. Soon, a crowd of about fifty formed a semi-circle around the entrance.

'Ready, Mills?' the huntsman called.

Velvet was shaky but back on her feet. The two foxes stood motionless in the darkness, facing the entrance. They had retreated as far back as they could go along the winding passage. They were now ten metres from the entrance.

It was Torn Ear who smelt the terrier first. He shivered. He knew that the dog had come to betray them. He pushed past Velvet and met it half-way along the main passage. The dog stopped. Uncertain. Its eyesight was not as good as the fox's and it was pitch black. It bared its teeth and growled. Then it started to bark.

Up on top, Mills heard it too. He gave a grunt of

satisfaction and got down on his hands and knees. He cupped an ear to the ground. He listened intently, then looked up at the watching crowd.

'They're under here,' he told them with a grin. 'All bottled up nicely.' He got up and brushed the damp earth from his knees.

'Reckon we'll start digging, then.'

Torn Ear and the terrier faced each other and all the time the dog never stopped barking. It went on and on. An hysterical yapping that drove Torn Ear mad with frustration. He attacked the dog in rage but it always managed to keep just out of reach.

Torn Ear wondered what the men were doing. The sudden thump of spades overhead gave him his answer. The sound of the blades slicing though the ground distracted the dog for a fraction of a second. But it was enough.

Torn Ear seized it by the nose, its most sensitive part, and a furious fight broke out. The passage was cramped and there was no room to manoeuvre. The terrier managed to tear itself free and retreated, yelping in pain.

Overhead, the spades crashed down. Fear closed in on Torn Ear. He had dug out enough young animals from their burrows and nurseries to know what was happening. He thought of the rats he had pinned against the wall of the mill and knew it wouldn't be very long before Velvet and he suffered the same fate.

He also remembered there was a badger sett nearby, which ran deep into the hillside. An old boar had been living there when Torn Ear first came. He had even moved in there when the badger left. In the end, he decided he didn't like the smell. The entrance to the sett was quite close. If he could only reach it . . . He pressed his nose to the ground in concentration.

Above him, the men crowded round as the dog emerged. Its muzzle was ripped to the bone by the fox's teeth. Blood streamed across its face and fell in heavy drops on the churned-up ground. A gasp went up.

'Never mind her,' called Mills. 'Don't need dogs no more. Be through any minute!'

There had to be a way out. Torn Ear was sure of it. He squeezed past Velvet and hurried back to the end of the passage. Frantically, he started to dig. His paws scrabbled at the sides of the tunnel, sending sheets of earth flying behind him. He battered at it with his head, desperate to force a way through. Earth clogged his eyes and nostrils.

The side of a spade sliced through into the tunnel just above Velvet's head. She shrank back. For an instant she saw the cold gleam of steel, then it was pulled clear. Earth spattered down on top of her.

At the same moment, Torn Ear's paws broke through a side wall and before he could stop himself, he was sliding head-first down into another passage. Velvet scrambled after him.

Behind them came a faint cheer of triumph.

Torn Ear drove himself forward, aware that the men were jumping down into the hole. They could only be a metre or two away at the most. The tunnel forked and he chose the left-hand passage. It twisted and turned and soon forked again. He put his nose to each exit and thought he could just feel a faint current of air through one of them.

Muffled shouts and the thump of more digging came from behind them. Another dog started to yap. It sounded quite close, though somewhere above them. The foxes scrambled on.

The tunnel grew narrower, pressing down on their heads and backs. Soon they were slithering along on their bellies, hardly able to use their front paws. And then an old tree root blocked the way ahead of them.

Torn Ear bunched his back legs under him and threw himself forward. He jack-knifed his body from side to side and kicked and fought to get a purchase on the uncaring ground. The pads on his paws became raw and the air was full of dust and drifting sand. Velvet sneezed and they lay rigid with fear in case the dog had heard.

It grew increasingly hot and they became desperate for water. They couldn't swallow, as their tongues and throats were coated with sand, and their eyes were gummed. In the distance, the noise of the hunt began to die. Then there were just the two of them and only the laboured effort of their own breathing.

Eventually, Torn Ear dug a way round. He pulled himself past the root and collapsed. For what seemed a long time he was happy to lie stretched out and sleep. It was the persistent current of cold, sweet air that made him get back on his feet. As they crawled along the passage, the current grew stronger. They could smell damp leaves and grass and felt suddenly exhilarated.

It was raining hard and the hunt had long since gone home when Torn Ear cautiously looked out from between the roots of an oak tree. Velvet joined him. The sound of rain pattering on the sodden ground greeted them like applause. But they waited there without moving until the darkness fell.

Sixteen

They walked a long way that night. Along the river bank, where they slipped into the water and felt new strength returning. Past the old mill where the rats were busy. Then up, over the fields, through the wood where they had first met and down the other side.

They skirted the cottage where Mills lived. Lights were burning in the downstairs rooms. In one of them, a television flickered blue behind the curtains.

Torn Ear smelt the terriers lying in their baskets beside the back door. He knew their stomachs were full and heard one of them yawn drowsily. There was a creaking as it settled down to sleep. Silently, the fox stopped at the wrought iron front gate and raised a leg.

They reached Velvet's earth at last and went

inside. It was dry and roomy and felt warm out of the wind. Too tired even to eat, they lay back-to-back like dogs, enjoying the warmth that seeped through their bodies. The pain of the day was already beginning to ease.

They woke many hours later. Overnight, a subtle change had occurred in both of them. As he looked out into the morning, Torn Ear felt a new confidence in himself and in his own strength. He had been brave where others would have slunk away. He had risked everything and he had won. He left the earth without waiting to see if Velvet was following and almost at once picked up a rabbit scent.

Velvet too felt differently. She had had no real dealings with Man before and having been so close to death had shocked her. Her days as a cub were over. From now on she would be more cautious, more alert, more suspicious. It was a good lesson to learn so early in life.

They spent all day together, running through the bare woods and bleak fields where flurries of snow stung their eyes. Between them, they caught two rabbits and a thrush that Velvet snatched from a low branch. They found a colony of leather-jackets under an old log and greedily crunched them up.

When they were full, they went back to the earth and lay close together, happy in the other's company. The need to play together like cubs was gone.

Two night later Velvet made Torn Ear leave. She did so with a sudden snarl and a baring of fangs. Strange new emotions were stirring inside her as the madness of mating approached.

She meant him no harm. She was just obeying the instincts Nature had given her. When her time came, she would select the strongest and most wise of all her suitors. In that way, her cubs would have a better chance of survival. Until the moment she summoned each of them to her, she would want to be on her own.

That time was not long in coming. The following day, Torn Ear was padding along a well-worn rabbit path when a familiar scent stopped him. It was freshly-made and threatening. Torn Ear's lips drew back in a snarl. Velvet's other companion, the old dog fox, had returned.

He bristled in rage and felt a violent hatred towards the stranger gathering inside him. He found Velvet's scent many times during the next week. On almost every occasion, it had been covered by the stranger.

But it wasn't until the night of the storm that the terrible fire consumed him. That was when he heard Velvet calling for a mate.

It was a scream tossed high on the wind. A summons he had never heard before. A terrible piercing cry that made his blood turn to ice. He knew at once what it meant. It rang inside his brain until his head felt it would burst open. A wildness possessed him and he ran towards the call.

To human ears, it sounded like a woman beside herself in agony, only louder, much louder. For Torn Ear, it was a command as old as Nature itself. He put his head back and howled out his love for her. As he stopped to draw breath, he thought he heard his rival do the same.

Seventeen

It was a night when the wind roared through the wood like a mad thing. It ripped through the tops of the great trees, breaking off branches and flinging them to the ground. It was impossible to face into. It tried to lift Torn Ear off his feet and send him pitching head-first into the darkness.

It was as the storm reached a crescendo that he found her. Velvet suddenly stepped out from behind a tree and stood directly in his path. It was a deliberate act. On a night like this, he could have passed by a metre away and not known she was there.

She danced up on her hind legs to greet him. They wrestled and swayed together, biting at each other's ears and rubbing their heads together. Torn Ear was dizzy with happiness and although his cries of delight were whipped away by the wind, she knew they were there.

And then all of a sudden, Velvet was struggling to get free and pushing him away. She bared her teeth in fear and dropped to the ground. She began to squirm away from him, dragging her body along the ground in submission.

A large dog fox stepped forward. He was lean and rangy and over a metre long from nose to tail. He ignored Velvet who was cowering in front of him. His eyes never left Torn Ear.

He came closer. Every movement full of menace. His muzzle was grey and pitted and he walked with a limp in a back leg. He began to circle round.

Torn Ear snarled at him, his throat full of the stuttering barks of hate. He showed his teeth and gestured with his head. The stranger whipped round and came leaping at him. The next moment, the two foxes were locked together in a spitting, biting fury.

The fox slashed at Torn Ear's muzzle, just missing his eye. Torn Ear threw his head back out of the way and the next instant the stranger had him by the throat. His teeth bit down, pulling Torn Ear over on his back.

They toppled and fell heavily. Torn Ear, although

smaller, was strong-boned and approaching his prime. As they landed he managed to get a foot up into the older male's stomach and bring it raking down. The stranger gasped in pain and relaxed his grip sufficiently for Torn Ear to shake himself loose.

They stood and faced each other some body-lengths apart, sucking in great gulps of air. The stranger seemed to recover quicker and came at Torn Ear again, this time in a sideways barging movement that caught Torn Ear by surprise.

Torn Ear staggered back, and for once his sure-footedness deserted him. His feet slipped on the wet ground and the next moment he was fighting to stay on his feet. The big male screamed in triumph, seized him by the back of the neck and tried to shake him like a rat.

His teeth were like a vice. Torn Ear jerked and twisted round, struggling to throw him off. But the older fox was too experienced for him. The back of Torn Ear's head was wet with the old fox's saliva.

Torn Ear staggered. The stranger was falling on top of him, driving the air from his lungs. The weight was unbearable and the pain in his chest crushing. Torn Ear was fighting for breath, the blood roaring in his ears. He had to breathe or die.

Claws scraped down the side of his face and across the soft skin of his nose. Torn Ear jerked his head away and in the same instant saw his chance. He seized the other's front leg. He took it deep between his jaws and bit down hard. He hung on with all the strength he still had, grinding at the bone. The old dog screamed and slashed at Torn Ear's eyes with his other paw, fighting to break that grip.

Torn Ear heard his screams and bit even deeper. There was blood now in his eyes. It was hot and blinding and he knew it must be his own. Still he hung on. The weight on his chest eased and he knew the stranger was trying to get away.

Sensing the advantage, Torn Ear rolled to one side. Now he was on his feet and the stranger was backing away, holding the damaged leg tight against his side.

Torn Ear stood swaying for a long moment while he gathered his senses. Then he launched himself at the other. Their heads clashed and they were rolling over and over. Torn Ear felt the stranger flinch and turn away. In a flash, Torn Ear realised he was trying to protect his front leg.

His blood sang in triumph. He had beaten this

stranger and he knew it. He decided it was time to use a little bit of cunning.

Torn Ear pretended he was giving up and began to back away. He let his head hang and body droop in dejection. He looked a beaten animal.

The old fox screamed at him in derision.

Torn Ear dragged himself away as if in great pain. He stopped to lick his wounds. This was too big a temptation. With Velvet watching from the sides, the stranger came scrambling over to drive Torn Ear away for ever.

Torn Ear timed it well. He waited until the older fox was almost on top of him, then spun round, ducking under the other's body and seizing the wounded leg in his mouth. Velvet watched in total unconcern as the stranger screamed in agony. Torn Ear eventually released him.

As the old fox hobbled away, there was a brilliant flash of lightning and for an instant Velvet's eyes glowed red. The next moment, the air hissed and crackled and smelt of burning. The thunder-clap that followed could be heard even above the wind.

Then the madness seized Torn Ear and he was running for his life with no idea where he was going. All he knew was that Velvet was beside him, running with him. His legs were numb beneath him. Somehow, he drove them on.

Great stabs of lightning chased them through the wood as they ducked through the undergrowth. Thunder followed at their heels, terrifying them still further.

They hid in a ditch under an old wall and shivered and screamed at the storm until the worst of it was over. When they came out into the open, it was Velvet who took the lead and Torn Ear who followed. She ran towards her earth, ignoring him. When they got there, she snapped at him as he went to go inside.

Bewildered, Torn Ear lay on the ground staring at the entrance. It grew colder and more overcast. All the next day, Torn Ear waited there. His eyes never once left the entrance to Velvet's earth. Towards evening, it began to snow. Still he kept his vigil, until many hours after she had gone to ground, Velvet reappeared.

By now, she was hungry. Without so much as a glance at him, she swung off through the wood, scanning the freshly-fallen snow for likely tracks. Torn Ear followed ten metres behind.

He watched her feed on a rabbit she had caught,

and edged closer. His body was shaking with love for this beautiful vixen with the dainty black paws. Very daringly, he reached out a paw and touched her back. She whirled round and snarled at him. Meekly, he backed away.

All night long he followed her and all night long Velvet ignored him. He called to her, crooning softly, though all the time his eyes blazed with passion.

She led him across an open field where the snow had begun to drift up against the hedgerows. And there she turned and with her ears flat against her head, came running at him.

Before he could move, Velvet had jumped high over his head, flicking at him with her paws as she went. He spun round and gave chase, delighted with her new-found playfulness.

She tore round the field jinking left or right whenever he got too close, teasing him, daring him to catch her.

He skidded after her, sending the snow whirling high into the night. A solitary owl watching them from a tree, put its head on one side, puzzled by their antics.

Like dogs, they raced round the field, never

seeming to tire. Although it looked like play, it was in fact the final test for Torn Ear. Velvet was not going to surrender easily. It was for Torn Ear to anticipate and outrun her.

And he did. He was a body-length behind and running strongly. Somehow he knew she was going to spin right round and dodge past him.

Torn Ear leapt high into the air a fraction of a second before she made her move. He landed cat-like on all four legs across her path. She tried to spin away to one side to avoid him. But it was too late. She cannoned into him and they both tumbled over.

Velvet stood up and faced him, her tail lashing from side to side. She let him approach her, then leapt up and boxed him away, all the time making strange squealing noises.

But this time he was too quick for her. He seized one of her ears in his teeth and held it until she became calmer. Then, quite slowly, he mounted her and his entire being dissolved with love for her.

When it was finished, they went back to Velvet's earth and slept contentedly while outside the snow covered everything in a silent white blanket.

Eighteen

For the next eight weeks, Torn Ear never left her side. They hunted together during the long winter nights and he showed her the best places to watch from. She remembered the quarry where she had been born and wondered if it would make a better place to bring up her cubs. But when they got there, they found fresh traces of humans, and they left soon afterwards.

Towards the end of February, they learnt how to catch hares. Torn Ear had often tried to in the past, with no success. The hare had been too quick for him. Recently, they had both seen hares sitting bolt upright in a ploughed field.

Torn Ear and Velvet decided to lay an ambush for them. In the middle of an afternoon, while it was still light, Velvet trotted across to the middle of the field.

There was no sign of the hares. She stood motion-less for a little while then began to walk round in a small circle.

Torn Ear watched from cover and after five minutes or so, saw a sudden movement at one end of the field. It was a hare curious to see what Velvet was doing. He watched it come closer, its grey-brown coat blending perfectly with the ground.

Velvet continued to pace round looking neither one way or the other.

The hare came nearer. Silently, with infinite patience, Torn Ear crept round to get behind the hare, who by this time was openly sitting up and staring at Velvet. Torn Ear began to move towards it.

It started to rain and the daylight faded. It was time to act. The hare was now only thirty metres from Velvet. Torn Ear loped towards it. Almost at once, the hare's ears twitched, but it delayed looking round for a second too long.

When it did so, Torn Ear was racing towards it. The hare gave a scream and bolted and found Velvet coming straight towards it. It screamed again, a long thin cry that suddenly ended.

Velvet carried the limp carcass home and divided

it between them. Torn Ear thought it the best meat he had ever tasted.

Then came the time three weeks later when Velvet refused to leave the earth. Torn Ear stood beside her and made little whimpering noises of concern. But she lay on her side with her eyes closed and ignored him. She refused to eat the cock pheasant he had brought her and this worried him.

The bird had been winged on a recent shoot. It had spent the last two days hiding in a thicket of young trees, slowly dying of thirst. He picked the bird up again and dropped it beside her head to attract her attention. She raised her head, snarled briefly at him and closed her eyes again. Torn Ear turned and left, knowing it was best to leave her alone if that was what she wanted.

He lay down at the foot of a tree and waited. Later, when a frost began to form he tucked his head under his brush and dozed.

Much later still, he heard sounds that sent a shiver through him. There were faint cries and squeakings and the sound of Velvet purring in pleasure. He hesitated at the entrance to the earth, unsure whether to go in or not. Velvet heard and called him.

She raised her head in greeting, then lay back to

show him their cubs. There were five of them. Five black, curly-haired little creatures the size of newborn kittens. They lay packed together with their noses buried deep into their mother's side.

The air was full of contented murmurings and the sound of five hungry cubs enjoying their first meal.

There were three vixens and two dog cubs. Velvet licked them and nuzzled them and felt the glow of total contentment overwhelm her. She began to whimper in happiness.

Torn Ear gazed down at them, helpless with pride. He studied them all in turn, noting their sturdy little limbs and the greedy way they fed. They were all blind and would remain so for the next two or three weeks.

He looked at Velvet and grinned. Then he turned and went racing into the night to find her food.

Sixteen days later, Snape, the eldest of the vixens, had both eyes fully open. They were a brilliant blue and looked far too big for her pudgy, unformed face. She was the biggest and most active of the cubs. She was always the first to feed and did not hesitate to shoulder aside any of her brothers or sisters who got in her way.

By contrast, Brin, the younger dog cub, was the weakest member of the litter and several days behind Snape in his development. His eyes were still tight shut and he had the most difficulty getting enough to eat.

Velvet tried to treat all her cubs equally. They were washed several times a day. As they grew bigger, they protested loudly and tried to wriggle away. Velvet soon found the best way to deal with this was to pin them down with a heavy foot and lick them twice as hard.

Snape was the most difficult cub to catch. At three weeks old, she would back away from Velvet into the lowest corner of the earth. When Velvet hooked a paw in to pull her out, she would bare her tiny, baby teeth and scream defiance.

The cubs were fascinated by the world outside the earth. At four weeks old, the bravest of them started sitting in the darkness staring up at the light coming in. Day by day they grew bolder and crept nearer the entrance. It was a place of mystery for them. Frightening too, when the owls hooted overhead. There were strange new scents and unknown sounds to be wondered at.

One night not long afterwards, Snape and Ketto,

the elder male cub, ventured further than they had ever done before and tumbled down the steep slope outside the earth. Above them the other cubs stared down, wide-eyed at their boldness.

The next day, Torn Ear came back from hunting and brought them their first solid meal. It was a field mouse. He dropped it in front of them and went to look for Velvet.

The cubs stared at it for a long time, not knowing what to make of it. The mouse smelt of fresh blood. Snape crouched down and flicked it with her paw. She leapt back and waited to see what would happen. When nothing did, Ketto joined her and they both crept closer.

She touched it again, this time quite firmly. The mouse continued to lie still. Ketto scooped it up into the air and Snape made a grab for it. She missed and fell over. The next moment they both seized an end and were tugging at it. Their needle-like teeth punctured the skin and they tasted blood for the first time.

They pushed and struggled for possession, their throats full of baby growls. Neither of them knew how to eat the mouse. They avoided the body because the fur there tickled their nostrils and made them sneeze. Instead, they chewed at the soft little ears and the bare, stumpy tail.

It wasn't until Torn Ear bit the mouse in two that they began to understand. Behind them, three small heads looked down from the entrance and wailed for their mother.

Nineteen

The cubs were growing rapidly. Torn Ear lay in the grass and let them play over him. Five metres away, Velvet dozed in the warm May sunshine. The cubs raced between the two of them, trying to be the first to sit on their parents' heads and then defend their place against the rest.

Snape and Ketto, being the biggest, nearly always won. But there was still a great deal of tussling and screeching, with all the cubs rolling off and clambering back up Velvet and Torn Ear's sides.

Torn Ear took it all in good part and twitched his ears to show the cubs that he was enjoying it too. Brin, who was not as keen as the others on their version of 'King of the Castle', was playing a different game.

He was stalking the tip of Torn Ear's tail. He

began as far away as he could in the long grass in front of the ditch. Every time Torn Ear flicked the end of his brush, Brin froze in his tracks. When the brush was still again, he crept up on it.

Ignoring the others, he got to within a body-length of Torn Ear, then sprang high into the air and landed on the brush. Torn Ear woke with a yelp as sharp little teeth bit into his tail. He swatted Brin with a paw and scrambled up. The others fell off and rounded in a gang on Brin. His cries woke Velvet, who scolded them all and picked Brin up by the scruff and dropped him down beside her.

Watching the cubs lick blood from a rabbit carcass one evening, Torn Ear decided it was time the cubs learnt how to catch their own food. They were six weeks old and no longer helpless. They had shed their black baby fur and now had proper brown coats growing in. Their eyes were almost entirely yellow in colour and their muzzles were growing straight and pointed.

In the next few weeks they would grow even more rapidly, until by the end of July they would be almost fully-grown and able to fend for themselves. Before that though, he would leave them and Velvet too, and return to his own solitary life.

He would not seek out Velvet until the madness ran through his blood again. But until he left, he would defend these cubs as Nature intended him to. He called to Velvet to look after them, and shaking Ketto off again, trotted away. Torn Ear had remembered the old mill and the rats. It was time he paid them a visit.

Velvet uttered a short bark. The cubs immediately stopped playing and hugged the ground. They stayed where they were until she whistled for them to follow her. She took them down to the meadow. Yesterday, she had noticed a pair of thrushes teaching their babies how to fly. It was time the cubs learnt more about birds.

Velvet lay under a bush, the cubs on either side of her. She was teaching them how to listen. For the foxes, the air was full of the sounds of mice. In the grass all round them, they could hear the familiar squeakings and rustlings. But it was not this she was waiting for.

Silently, she made them look up into the branches of the tree opposite. The cubs saw the parent birds flying to and fro. They noted the bright, encouraging cries they made, which were quite different from the thrush song they were used to hearing.

Then they noticed the fledglings sitting uncomfortably along a branch, and connected the two facts. After a wait, one of the baby birds made a jump, and in a frantic beating of wings, landed safely on a lower branch. The cubs listened to the fluttering sound of the fledgling's wings, so different from the steady beat of its parents.

The next bird to try was not so lucky and landed beak-first on the ground. The parents fussed over it, while the bird kept its wings outstretched and tried to run to the safety of the tree. Its legs were not very strong so it kept falling over. This was the other sound Velvet particularly wanted them to hear and understand. It told them that here was an easy meal for the taking.

She waited until two more fledglings were on the ground, then told the cubs to catch them. She listened to them squabbling over the kills and was pleased. She watched Snape run off with one of the birds in her jaws. Ketto started to follow, then realised there were easier pickings closer to hand. He ran back.

Torn Ear heard some of the cubs fighting and turned back to look. He was some distance above them, walking along the higher ground above the meadow.

A sixth sense alerted him and he froze. A second later, two boys appeared over the brow of the hill, They were riding mountain bikes and swept past him going very fast.

The boys were the Johnson twins – Phillip and Dan, aged twelve. They were out on their usual Saturday morning ride. They had rucksacks stuffed with crisps, a meat pie, a bar of chocolate and some orange juice on their backs.

Torn Ear was not too worried. Velvet would also have seen the humans and have the cubs close to her. It would only take a moment for them all to slip away unseen. Even so, he was surprised how quickly the boys were covering the ground.

He saw the boys heading towards the bush and heard Velvet's sharp bark, warning the cubs of danger.

A flicker caught his eye and he stared in disbelief. It was Snape. She was cut off from Velvet and the others and was running in the open towards the safety of some long grass. The boys had seen her too. Torn Ear heard their whoops of excitement as they chased after her.

Had Snape been fully grown she would have easily outrun the bicycles. But she was not. She still only had a cub's stamina and speed.

The boys raced on either side of her for almost fifty metres. She must have stopped suddenly, intending to double back, but the boys were ready. They skidded to a halt and flung themselves down on top of her.

Torn Ear watched them struggling to hold her. One of the boys tore off his rucksack and shook out the contents. He pulled it down over Snape's head. The next minute, they were holding up the bag and shouting in triumph. Torn Ear's favourite cub was now a prisoner.

Twenty

The Johnsons lived in the same village where, months before, Velvet and Torn Ear had raided the orchard. Torn Ear shivered as he saw the gate and the ivy-covered tree where he had hidden. He had deliberately avoided the place since then. The memory of the nail in his paw was still vivid. But this was different. All his instincts demanded he must find Snape.

He followed the boys, which was easy enough to do. Snape was struggling like a mad thing inside the bag. There was no way either boy could cycle home carrying her on his back. She would have thrust her head up through the flap at the top of the bag and been out like a flash.

So they walked instead and both used one hand to keep the cub inside. Torn Ear followed like a shadow, not far behind.

The Johnsons lived in a stone cottage beside the farm. Both the parents worked there. Mrs Johnson had just returned from the village shop when her sons burst into the kitchen.

'A fox!' she exclaimed, when she at last made sense of what they were telling her. 'A fox? In that nice new bag I got you? I don't believe it!'

But she had to when they let her peep inside.

'It's only a cub,' Phillip told her. 'We can keep it, Mum, can't we?'

'Yeah! We'll look after it all right. Be no trouble, you see,' Dan added, tugging at her arm.

Their mother was not so sure. 'But there's nowhere to keep it!' she cried. 'What are we going to feed it on? It's a wild animal. No! Certainly not,' she snapped, shaking her head.

They begged and pleaded, until finally she said, 'Well, just for now then. Put it out in the old rabbit hutch in the garden. But only till your dad gets back. And mind it doesn't bite you,' she shouted after them. 'There's rabies and things!'

The boys bundled into the garden and dragged the old hutch on to the middle of a small piece of lawn. Wire-netting covered the front of it and inside there were a couple of pieces of shrivelled cabbage leaves. The bolt on the door slid open smoothly enough.

'You put that cage back where you got it,' Mrs Johnson ordered, coming out to see what they were doing. 'That's in the way of my washing right there.'

They pulled the hutch back to its original place at the foot of a high wall. The earth was damp where it had been standing. The boys slid Snape out of the bag and slammed the bolt home. Then all three of them squatted down in front of the cage and peered in.

'It's ever so cute,' said Mrs Johnson, with a break in her voice.

'Can we keep it then, Mum?' Dan demanded eagerly.

Mrs Johnson wavered. 'Well . . . No! Like I said. Wait till your dad gets home and then we'll see.'

But when he returned for his lunch, Mr Johnson was not at all pleased with the news.

'Have you kids gone stark staring mad?' he demanded. 'There's geese and hens and I don't know what at the farm. That fox'll kill the lot of them if it gets out. Want me to lose my job or something?'

'We really can't afford to feed it, anyhow,' his wife added, feeling a little sorry for her sons. 'You'll just have to take it back to where you found it and let it go again.'

Mr Johnson looked at her. 'Fox like that's no good to anyone,' he said. 'I'll give old Brian Mills a call. He'll know what to do with it.'

He went inside the house to telephone. The others looked at Snape, who was backed up in a corner snarling at them.

'Now, what did I say,' Mrs Johnson told them. 'See there! It's a wild animal. Lord knows what it won't do!'

'Oh Mum! We'd look after it . . . promise,' they chorused.

'That's all right then,' said Mr Johnson, coming back out into the tiny garden. 'His wife says he'll be over later on. He's a bit tied up this afternoon.' He frowned at his sons. 'You keep a good eye on it till he gets here. Understand? Only he doesn't want it getting out. Vermin he calls it. And I agree with him. Now, where's my dinner? I'm starving.'

Twenty One

Torn Ear watched Mr Johnson return home for lunch. He was hiding in a ditch opposite. A little later he saw him go back to work. The man walked down the concrete path that ran along the side of the cottage. He slammed the side gate behind him and strode off down the road, looking angry.

The distance between Torn Ear and the side gate was too great for the fox to risk crossing in broad daylight. Instead, he made his way round under cover to the rear of the cottage where he found a tumbledown shed. He leapt up on to its roof and from there on to the wall that ran behind the Johnsons' garden. An overhanging tree gave him good cover.

Cautiously, he picked his way along the top of the wall and stared down into the garden, two metres below. There was a small lawn which went up to the back of the cottage. Round the side, he saw the concrete path and the gate.

He noticed the hutch at once and at the same moment, caught Snape's scent. He called her name very quietly, so only she would know. He could hear the panic in her voice when she cried out for him to help.

Just then, the twins came out of the back door and Torn Ear sank down and remained motionless. The boys pushed bread through the wire mesh and pieces of cake. The sweet, sickly smell of humans made Snape feel ill. She shrank away. In any case, she was too frightened to eat. The only thing she needed was water, but this no one thought of giving her.

Mrs Johnson came out to join her sons and spent a lot of time bending over and talking to the cub. Snape by now was almost paralysed with fear at their ugly human faces and the black holes of their mouths. She cowered in the back of the rabbit hutch, clinging to the hope that Torn Ear was close by.

Still later, Mr Johnson appeared. He was scowling and grumbling about the state of the milking parlour. After tea, he watered the garden with a hose-pipe. A spray of water splashed across Snape's cage and she screamed and leapt back as if scalded. Mr Johnson laughed and did it again until his sons shouted at him to stop.

A small dog wandered out into the next door garden. It stopped and looked up at the wall. For a moment it stood still, sniffing the air. Then it caught Torn Ear's scent. It began to bark. When its owner came to see what the noise was about, the dog began to jump up at the wall.

Luckily, the human was too busy with her own concerns to bother about the dog's behaviour. She caught it by the collar and dragged it away.

All this time Torn Ear watched. The stones on the top of the wall were hard and unyielding under his body and he was stiff and uncomfortable.

The sun had begun to sink before the Johnsons went indoors. A telephone rang inside the house. Carefully, Torn Ear got up and took a tentative step. The next moment, he stopped and almost cried out with pain. Pins and needles gripped his legs.

For a full three minutes he could not move. Never had time taken so long to pass. When the circulation returned, he jumped down unsteadily into the

Johnsons' garden and ran over to the cage. Snape gave a yelp of joy, then threw her weight against the sides of the hutch, banging into them, trying to batter her way out.

He tried to calm her but she was too panic-stricken to listen. Torn Ear glanced at the back door. It was open. At any moment one of the humans might hear the noise Snape was making and come to investigate.

He waited, poised for flight. The seconds ticked by. Far away, he heard the whine of an engine on the evening air. It was a sound he recognised, though he was too distracted now to remember where he had last heard it.

He started to dig furiously in front of the hutch, attacking the ground with his front paws, reaching deep into the soft earth and spraying it behind him in a heavy shower. The hole deepened. Seeing what he was doing, Snape began to do the same.

The noise of the vehicle grew louder. It was entering the village. Torn Ear's paws struck against something hard and unyielding. He redoubled his efforts. It was a brick and it was lying directly in his way.

A wave of frustration swept him. He tried to bite

it and kill it. Then his brain told him to dig round it. He remembered the humans and snatched a quick glance. No sign of them. A gust of laughter from the television filtered out into the garden.

The brick moved and he dug even harder. It slipped to one side. Now he could drag it clear. Above him, Snape was digging furiously to meet him.

A Land Rover pulled up outside the cottage. Through the wooden slats of the side gate, Torn Ear saw its tail lights gleam. Then they went out.

There were voices. Loud men's voices and the excited chatter of children. There was something else. A familiar scent that brought sudden terror to Torn Ear and made him stop what he was doing.

Dogs! But not just any dogs. He knew that scent too well. It meant death.

His paw broke through into the hole that Snape was digging. Now the cub was crying in delight. Torn Ear dug and dug, too frightened to do anything else. He tore at the small opening in front of him. His mouth and nostrils were full of earth. He could hardly breathe. Still he dug. His life and the life of his cub depended on split seconds of time.

He felt Snape's paws scraping against his muzzle.

Ten seconds later, he seized her and backed out of the hole as fast as he could, dragging her with him.

Men's voices were approaching. Heavy boots scraped on the concrete path. A gate squeaked on dry hinges.

But by then, Torn Ear held Snape by the scruff of her neck. He turned to face them. Five seconds earlier and he could have raced past them through the side gate. They would never have caught him.

Mr Johnson saw him first.

'What the heck!' he shouted but Mills the gamekeeper was already pushing past him and running towards the fox. He raised the stick he carried up over his shoulder. Behind him, the dogs were barking, their paws slipping on the concrete in excitement.

There was no way out. The men and dogs blocked the pathway. The foxes were trapped in Mr Johnson's little garden. Unless . . . unless . . .

Torn Ear looked back at the wall, measuring its height. He took a deep breath and crouched with his stomach brushing the ground. Then with every muscle in his body stretched to breaking point, he sprang for the top of it, two metres above his head.

The stick hit the wall beside him. A hand grabbed

at his tail. But by then he had got his front paws on top. His back legs kicked frantically. The men were shouting. Another blow from the stick caught him full across his back.

Torn Ear gasped. The pain was intense. For a second, he began to slip. His legs scrabbled in desperation against the wall. He pulled himself up, centimetre by centimetre. Snape was screaming as he heaved again.

The men were beside themselves with anger. There was noise and violence all round. Another blow from the stick, but he scarcely felt it. Then he had pulled his head and shoulders over and was half-falling down the long drop on the other side.

He landed lightly on all fours and listened to the impotent rage of the men and their dogs and took a fresh grip on Snape. He turned and ran into the dusk. They were free! They had won!

He ran a full mile before he stopped and put Snape down. The cub nuzzled him and licked his face. Torn Ear's heart was full and he fussed over his cub, making sure she was not injured and well enough to continue.

Darkness was falling by then. From the middle of

the wood above the village, a nightingale began to pour her heart out on the warm night air. And all the while, Torn Ear waited and watched for any sign of pursuit.

When he was sure no dog or human was following, Torn Ear walked on. He did this to let Snape keep up with him. It was a good way of tiring the cub and driving out the memories of being imprisoned in that terrible hutch.

By the time they neared Velvet's earth, the cub was swaying on her feet with exhaustion. A hedgehog heard them approach and rolled itself into a tight ball. But Torn Ear ignored it. This was not the time to try and force open a hedgehog, delicious though its flesh was.

He barked once, then again, and several more times. For a moment he thought Velvet had left, taking the cubs with her. He ran on ahead, calling for her. Then he heard her whistle of surprise.

He raced through the trees and the undergrowth. Familiar places again. And yet, even at a time like this, Torn Ear felt his own restlessness return. Snape was safe again and he was glad. Soon though, she would be leaving to begin her own life. He might never see her again.

The need to be on his own was growing stronger every day. It was not that he didn't love Velvet. He did. And he would return and fight for her again when the snow and the madness returned.

But that was a long way in the future and he couldn't imagine life that far ahead. Now, what he wanted most was to lie in the tall grass and listen to the field mice scuttling underneath. He remembered cool woods in the moonlight and the smell of new places. There were some moorhens at the old mill he wanted to stalk. He would take Velvet there before he left and show her too.

He came out into the open and caught Velvet's scent on the air in front of him. He felt a sudden blaze of happiness spring up inside and ran faster, greedy to see her again. He knew he must leave, but was glad there was still a little time left.

And then she was by his side, crying over him and Snape, her lost cub. They were together again. And that was all that mattered.